Gage

Gage

An American Extreme Bull Riders Tour Romance

Katherine Garbera

TULE
PUBLISHING

Gage

ISBN: 978-1-947636-38-5

Prologue

GAGE POWELL WAS tired as he pulled his rental car onto the driveway of his parents' ranch in southeast Oklahoma. He'd left Edinburgh, Scotland, at 11 a.m. yesterday, flown for sixteen hours to Dallas and then rented a car to drive…home.

But it hadn't felt like home in a long time. Certainly not seven years ago when his older brother Marty had taken his last ride on a bull called Blue Manchu and been trampled and gored to death. It had been horrifying to watch as Gage had stood next to the chute waiting for his debut on the Professional Bull Riders Association Tour. He'd been unable to ride that day; instead he'd followed his brother's ambulance with his dad in a truck. While his mom had ridden with Marty.

Everything had changed that day. Before that Gage had been able to pretend that winning a bull-riding championship would finally earn his father's respect and maybe his dad would stop looking at him like he wished he weren't there. But that hadn't happened. In fact, his father had turned to him at the hospital after they'd been told that Marty had died and point-blank told him that the wrong son had died.

Gage had hugged his grieving mom and walked away from the hospital. It had been all he could do. He'd hitched a ride home, gotten his truck and threw a few of his things in a duffel bag and left. He'd made his way south to the Gulf Coast where he'd gotten a job on an oil rig and eventually a transfer to one of the big rigs off the coast of Scotland. It paid well and was about as damn far away from bull riding as a man could get.

He'd been back to the States once a year since then meeting his mom for a week in Dallas and lately driving down to Whiskey River, Texas, to visit with Nicholas Blue, his brother's best friend, and to practice bull riding.

And that had been enough for him. His dad hadn't wanted to see him and frankly Gage didn't give a rat's ass if he ever laid eyes on the old man again.

Or so he'd thought.

His mom had emailed him while he was on the rig saying that he was needed back home. That his father's Alzheimer's was worsening and if he ever wanted a chance to see him and be recognized he needed to make his way home. Gage had been torn up about it. He was still mad at his dad. Not ready to forgive him for what he'd said in his pain and anger but there was still that damned little boy inside of him who wanted his father's approval, so here he was.

Sitting outside their house at what the hell time was it?

Four-thirty a.m.

Damn.

He just sat there trying to decide if he should turn the engine on and drive away but then the porch light came on and the front door opened.

Gage got out of the rental car and walked toward the house recognizing the figure of his father. He tensed.

"Son?"

"It's me, Dad," Gage said.

"Damn, boy, I've missed you," his father said.

Gage had never thought he'd hear those words from his father and admitted to himself as the old man walked to him and embraced him, he was glad he'd come home. He'd needed this.

"Your mom said you weren't going to make it," his father said, pulling back from the embrace. "But I told her Marty never lets me down."

Gage's heart sunk and he shook his head. He should've known better. When had his father ever been happy to see him?

"Um, I can't stay long."

"I know, boy," he said, clapping him on the back. "The American Extreme Bull Riders Tour is calling your name and this year you're going to win that buckle. I got a good feeling about it."

He wished it were as easy as his father made it sound. But that gold buckle wasn't going to be easy to get. He knew he'd be up against forty of the best guys in the world. And his dad—crap, his dad thought he was Marty. His dad thought he could get to the top, stay in the points and win it.

Staring over at his father in the inky shadowy light provided by the front porch, he realized something deep inside. His father was pretty far-gone and probably worse off than his mother had told him. He was never going to be the father Gage wanted him to be. Never. But he could be the son that his father wanted. He'd reached out to the tour organizers and because of his past experience he could ride this year as a rookie—a damned old one at twenty-five. He'd mentioned it to his mom, which he guessed was why his dad thought he was Marty.

If he let him think he was Marty and he rode in the competition, he could give his dad back the son he'd lost. And then when the tour was over and he'd won the championship he could go back his life far away from the rodeo, Oklahoma and his father.

Alicia Flores, the PR person for the AEBR, had decided he had the kind of story they could sell to the fans. Riding to continue his family's legacy, riding for his dead brother's memory. Riding to redeem himself in his father's eyes.

"I certainly am going to try to win it," he said at last.

"You'll do it, boy. That has to be why you're back," his father said.

He followed the old man up the stairs and into the house. The hands on their ranch were already hard at work. Gage didn't know if he'd made the dumbest decision of his life right then but it had been the only thing he could do.

He had always wanted to see his father smile at him the way he had done just a few moments ago. Something that had been elusive and out of his reach, and even though it might seem like a fool's errand—hell, it definitely was—it was one he was going to see through to the end.

Chapter One

S IERRA MONTEZ ROLLED her eyes as she heard her sister gushing over Cody Galen. It wasn't like the bull rider was even remotely interested in her. If Sierra had to guess it would be because Savanna had slept with him on last year's tour and Cody struck her as the kind of guy who kept moving forward.

She tucked a strand of hair that had escaped her ponytail back behind her ear, turning to search for the rookie rider who was supposed to be at the Fan Experience booth next.

Gage Powell.

She knew his history—everyone did. Supposed to make his debut seven years ago and slotted to ride right behind his older brother: a solid rider who'd had a lot of wins but never clinched the championship. And Marty Powell never would. The bull he'd drawn that day…well, everyone said it had been ornery, more so than Marty who'd like to fight. Marty had been thrown and his hand caught in the rope so he'd taken a beating from the bull as the animal tried to free himself of Marty.

Sierra had been sixteen and not at the rodeo that night

but her father had been watching it on the TV. She'd always remembered how they'd cut away to Gage, standing there waiting for his go, and the ashy color of his features as he'd climbed out of the chute and walked away.

He'd just turned and walked out of the rodeo and never looked back. Rumor had it he'd backpacked across Europe or had gone to Alaska and been driving a truck on the ice road. But no one had heard a word from him.

Until this year.

He'd shown up last fall at a local rodeo in Marietta, Montana, and then worked the smaller circuits until he had enough points to enter the American Extreme Bull Riders Tour. He'd been doing okay too. Getting in good solid rides. Yeah, she'd been following him. Unlike Savanna who went on the road with the tour, Sierra had spent most of the year in the corporate offices in Dallas. She was just joining the tour. And now Gage was back and making his debut.

She never let herself look at any of the bull riders the way that Savanna did. She was embarrassed by her older sister and the way she couldn't stop flirting with every one of them when they walked into the big tent that their family sponsored. But there had been something about Gage, which was why she'd only just now come to the fan event and visited the American Extreme Bull Riders Tour.

She'd been in her office in Dallas working her butt off, trying to prove to the board she'd deserved her job for her skills and not because she was a Montez. Plus she really couldn't resist Sacramento. It was a gorgeous city and her mom lived in San Francisco so she was combining her work trip with her daughterly duty.

Whatever it was she'd thought she'd seen in his eyes that night when his brother had been fatally injured…it had never let her stop thinking about him. It was warm on this August weekend but the temperature rose a bit when she saw him standing there.

He'd walked in, pulled off his sunglasses and scanned the air-conditioned tent. She walked over to him.

"Sierra Montez," she said, holding out her hand. "I'm in charge of the rookies this year."

Uh, great. She was acting like this was her first big job instead of something she'd been coordinating since she graduated nearly four years ago. This was crazy. *Act professional. He's just like any other guy.*

Except hotter.

And she never fantasized about any of the other bull riders. Only Gage.

"Nice to meet you, ma'am," he said, doffing his hat and smiling at her. Unlike some of the other bull riders his age or older, he didn't look beat up and broken.

"Same," she said. "We have the jeans we'd like you to wear over there in the dressing room. The fans love it if you leave your shirt off and…would you consider wearing a temporary tattoo with either your number or our logo on it?"

Everyone was different. Most of the rookies were young

kids who'd been waiting for this for their entire lives. They loved having the buckle bunnies lining up to get a picture with them—all with the knowledge that any of the rookies could be the next big thing on the American Extreme Bull Riders Tour.

"Sure. Whatever it is I'm supposed to do," he said.

He ducked behind the curtain and she stood outside watching his boots underneath the gap.

"I see you've picked yourself a rookie," Savanna said, coming up next to her.

"I haven't picked myself anything. I'm just doing my job. I'm the rookie liaison—you know that," Sierra said deliberately turning her back on the dressing area where Gage was. Her sister gave her a knowing smirk and Sierra didn't know how to respond.

She was still processing the fact that he'd looked even better in person than he had on TV and on the publicity photo that had been included in her packet. He'd smelled good too. Not overwhelmingly of cologne as some of the men who'd been in the tent did.

"He's not bad. I like 'em young."

"Of course you do," Sierra said.

"What's wrong with that?"

"Nothing. It's just—"

"You're saving yourself for Mr. Right?" Savanna asked.

The tone made her feel silly. What could she say? Maybe it was watching Savanna go through men like they were disposable or her own mama who was on her fifth husband that had made her shy. Sierra didn't know. She only knew that most of the men she met seemed too shallow and vapid. She didn't want to share any part of herself with someone who had one eye on the door.

"I'm not interested in some guy who's just marking time with me before he gets his next thrill on the back of a bull," she said. She walked away from her sister and to the area she'd set up earlier. Really there was nothing else for her to do, but if she had to listen to Savanna for another second she'd lose it.

The banner over the booth held the Montez Denim logo along with the backsides of all of this year's rookies on it. Underneath in bold red text read: The feel of the West.

She'd come up with it and they'd had a pretty good response, which had impressed her dad and the rest of the board. Working for a family-owned company had its drawbacks—like sometimes her father and uncles still saw her as a teenager, or worse a child, and didn't always want to give her the responsibility she could handle. She'd had to threaten to leave and take a job back East in order to get them to relent and give her this campaign.

She peeked around the curtain to see that there were already several fans in the queue. Not all of them were women though the majority were. She heard someone behind her and turned to see Gage standing there.

He had a faded chambray shirt on but had left the buttons open revealing his muscled chest and abs. He had their classic vaquero-cut jeans on. They were slim-fitting through the thighs but cut more generously at the bottom to fit easily over his boots, which were clearly a fancy pair. Hand-tooled dark leather with an intricate stitching design. She recognized the work as the Texas brand Kelly Boots from Whiskey River.

"I'm ready," he said. "Gotta get back to my next thrill."

SHE BLUSHED. LIKE legit turned pink before just shaking her head. "Sorry you heard that. My sister—"

"No way. Savanna is your sister?"

"Ha, you know she is," Sierra said.

He did know that. He had seen her at the first rookie/brand meeting back at the start of the AEBR Tour. She had worn a skirt and buttoned-up shirt. She reminded him of some of the oil company execs who'd used to visit once a year when he'd been working on the rigs. But younger. And prettier. And hotter.

"I do know. Just joshing with you. Why haven't we seen you on the tour before this?" he asked.

"Because some people are stubborn."

"Who?"

"The board. My father," she said. "But I'm here now so that's all that matters."

"Out-stubborned them, did ya?"

She smiled then and it lit up her entire face. "Yay."

"Good for you. That's me on every ride. Just determined to out-ornery every bull I get on."

She laughed. "You're doing pretty good this season."

"I'm doing all right," he admitted casually but there was nothing low-key about his ambition this year. He was back to win the Powell boys one more championship and to prove to himself he was just as good as his brother. It was hard living in Marty's shadow. His older brother had been the perfect son, good grades, first to do chores and he had been magic on the back of a bull. Marty could ride the spurs off anyone else as his mom liked to say and Gage had grown up half hero-worshiping his older brother and half resenting him.

Gage liked to think that if Marty hadn't died after his last ride maybe Gage would have matured enough to have a good relationship with him. He was close to Marty's best friend Nicholas Blue, which was what made him feel like it might have worked. But given their father, it was unlikely. He knew that.

"Ah, so you're in it for the gold buckle," she said.

"Anyone who tells you they ain't is lying. The truth is we all are riding for something. I'm riding to prove I'm as a good as—" What the hell? He hadn't planned to admit that. "Never mind. Where do you need me?"

She nibbled on her bottom lip for a moment and he

thought she wasn't going to let it go, but then she did. "Over here."

He followed her lead and let her position him in front of a large canvas sign that had a picture of Hammerfall on it with his head down.

"You'll need to lose the shirt. And what about the tattoo?" she asked. "I can get one of the assistants to put one on you. We're giving them away in the tent."

"Nah, I'm good," he said.

"Yes, you are," she said.

He arched an eyebrow at her. Now she sounded like her sister.

"Could you pretend you didn't hear that?"

"I could. But you know there's nothing wrong with my hearing," he said.

He took a half step closer to her and she held her hand up. She was funny and easy to rattle and cute and sweet so he stopped. He was going back to Scotland when this year was over. He was going to win the championship and then walk away from it all. Go out on top the way Marty should have instead of riding for one more shot at glory and dying.

His focus had to be the ride.

Not the girl with the brown ponytail and green eyes that made him think of a freshly mowed field in spring. The kind that had always tempted him to go and lie down in it. She licked her lips. They were full and a soft pink color that made him believe that kissing her would be…delicious. His own lips went dry at the thought of kissing her.

He stepped back and turned away. He needed to get this over with and get out of here. Back to his trailer so he could chill out and remember what he was doing this for. Focus had been the one thing he'd been able to take for granted as an adult. But suddenly she was messing with his.

No matter how luscious those lips looked, he knew better than to feed his own fantasies about her. He couldn't afford a distraction. Distracted men got bucked off their bull. Distracted men died.

He had plans to live a good long life.

"I'm ready," he said.

"Hey, sorry for being all lecherous just a second ago. I mean is there anything worse than sexual harassment in the workplace?"

"What you were doing wasn't sexual harassment. It's called attraction," he said. "And if I were any other guy I'd probably have taken you up on the offer."

"I wasn't offering," she said stiffly, turning to the curtain to open it.

"Whatever you say, darlin'."

SIERRA STOOD OFF to one side watching the women in the line flirting with Gage and him lapping it up like a starving man at a buffet. No wonder he thought he was God's gift to womankind. She tried to focus on being ticked off at him.

But to be honest focusing on the other women was all that was keeping her from drooling over him. He was gorgeous. She knew that. His muscles rock hard from years spent doing whatever it was he did. She knew bull riders had to be in shape but he'd been gone for seven years. Surely, he shouldn't still be this ripped—but he was.

He was arrogant.

Yeah, but what bull rider wasn't.

They came out of the womb swaggering and probably from the time he was in the nursery at the hospital women had been falling for his charm.

He'd called her darlin'. She shook her head.

"Dang, girl, you can deny it all you want but that man has your attention," Savanna said, coming up to her and draping her arm over Sierra's shoulder.

"Stop it. I'm not doing that. He's part of our brand and the fans seem to really like him," Sierra said, using her best professional tone. "That's as far as my interest goes."

"Why do you do that?" Savanna asked.

"What?"

"Deny yourself what you want? Do you think that it makes you better than me?"

She turned to look at her sister and felt petty about all the times she'd had been judgey about her. The truth was Savanna was very happy with her life and the choices she made.

"No. It doesn't," she admitted. "I just worked so hard to get the board to give me this AEBR campaign and I don't want to screw it up. Plus I've always been better at work than at play."

"Honey, Daddy isn't going to demote you because you flirt with a bull rider. If he does, I'll give him hell."

"That's not what I'm worried about. I want to be taken seriously by the board. Not just have them give me projects because I'm Dad's daughter. I worked hard to get my degree and my ideas are high concept. I don't want to ruin that because I couldn't keep my hands off of one of the rookies."

"I never can keep mine off," Savanna said. "But I can see that it's important to you. I'd offer to take him off your hands but he's not interested in me."

"He's not?" she asked. She didn't care… Okay, of course she cared. Every guy she knew was interested in Savanna. She drew men to her like fireflies at dusk. She just had something that most men couldn't resist.

"He told me so point-blank a few events back."

"Interesting. Maybe he has a no getting involved with sponsors policy," Sierra said.

"I doubt that man has a policy about women. If he wants one I'd say he'd go after her. I think there is more to him being here this year than we can guess. More to it than being a rookie."

"I think so too. You know about his brother," Sierra said.

"Yeah. I remember him. You were too young to be on

the tour, but Marty…he was special."

"Did you and he hook up?"

"No. I did with his friend Nicholas, but that's just the way Nick is. Marty was different. He was gifted on the back of a bull. Seemed like he was made to ride them."

"Yeah until he fell off," Gage said coming over to them.

"Sorry, Gage. I didn't realize you were standing there," Savanna said.

"My time is up. Came over to have a word with Sierra."

"Well I've got things to do," Savanna said, walking away.

Sierra turned to look at him. He'd put his shirt back on and was slowly doing up the buttons. "Sorry you had to hear that," Sierra said.

"What? Someone talking about my brother?" he asked.

"Yeah. I guess. I mean is it weird?"

"Yes and no. The hard part is that he's gone and because I haven't been around bull riders for the last few years it's making the accident fresh in everyone's mind," he said.

"Even in yours?" she asked then realized that might be too personal for two casual acquaintances.

"Sometimes," he said. "My mom is going to be coming to see me ride in Dallas. Could I get some tickets for her through you?"

"Yes. We have the VIP viewing stand as well. Just give me her details and I'll get it all set up."

"Thanks," he said turning and walking away.

She watched him the entire time until he was gone.

She'd like to say that her crush on the TV version of Gage hadn't stood up to the real man but that would be a lie. In person, he was more dynamic. His eyes were pale gray and she realized how expressive they were by what he hadn't shown. And though she knew it had to be a tough memory losing his brother, he'd revealed none of that to her while she'd been talking to him.

But it was only when he'd mentioned his mom that she saw any flash of emotion…that and when he'd been teasing her.

Which she had to admit she liked a little too much.

If she'd been Savanna she would have run right after him and asked him out. But she wasn't Savanna. She never would be. Though she thought it was being smart that kept her solidly standing in her place, she knew it was fear. Fear that Gage might be more than just a crush to her while she'd be nothing more than a buckle bunny and a quick hookup to him.

Chapter Two

GAGE KNEW HE should be in bed. He had to ride well on Saturday morning to qualify and make it to the finals on Saturday night, but he was restless. It didn't help that his dad had called him to give him some advice for tomorrow. He'd been watching the bulls throughout the tournament and had advice on each one that Harper breeders had provided.

He'd listened to all of his father's notes and then talked to his mom who had that sad note in her voice as she'd thanked him for letting his dad think he was Marty and listening to him yammer on—his mom's words—about the bulls.

Gage had felt like he always did: a little bit like an idiot and a little bit happy deep inside. His father had won the PBR championship buckle three times back in the '80s. Back before the sport had been mainstream and was only televised on some local stations. So his father knew what he was talking about when it came to riding and staying on. He'd been the one to teach Marty and Marty had taught him.

Gage had always looked up to Marty and it wasn't until

he'd started junior rodeo that he'd realized the difference in the way their father treated them. The difference—hell, that was a destructive line of thinking.

He had a bottle of whiskey under the sink in his trailer and he was about to open it up and forget, but that wasn't the smartest thing for a man who had a ride first thing in the morning. Instead he grabbed his Stetson and left the trailer, walking fast, looking at the stars, wondering if his brother was getting one last good laugh in at his expense.

"Uh, eek."

The words registered just as he plowed into someone. He grabbed the other person, felt his hand brush over a breast and looked down into those big green eyes that he recognized. Sierra. She had let her hair down from her ponytail and it hung around her shoulders.

"Sorry."

"It's okay," she said.

He let his hand slide down her waist and remembered that moment earlier when she'd been watching his mouth and he'd seen something in her eyes that had tempted him to lean in and kiss her. But he'd hesitated.

Tonight, though, with the demons of his past hot on his heels, he couldn't understand why he hadn't just taken the kiss she clearly wanted. He definitely needed to distract himself.

He slid his hand further around her body to the small of her back and she looked up at him, her lips parted and her head tipped to the side.

"Gage?"

"Hmm," he said, but really, he wasn't listening to anything she said. He was watching that mouth of hers with the full lower lip and realizing he needed—needed—to know how it felt under his. He started to lower his head and she licked her lips.

She put her hands on his shoulders, a light feathery touch that he felt all the way down to the base of his spine. Their lips met and she sighed a little, as she opened hers under his. His slipped his tongue inside and she tasted of strawberries and wine, he thought, and something else. Something unique.

Her hands tightened on his shoulders as she went on her tiptoes and leaned in to him. The brush of her breasts against his chest made his heart beat faster. He kept his touch light. His mind was spinning, thinking this was what he needed. That he should break the kiss and lead her back to his trailer and then spend the rest of the night twisting with her on the sheets; but when he lifted his head, he saw her eyes were closed and she licked her lips and then smiled slightly before opening them.

She was sweet.

Too sweet for him to use her to forget. He knew that. But he didn't want to let her go. He was doing something that made him feel like a saint some days and others like a sinner who would never get redemption.

"Gage?"

"Hell."

"Not hell. That was…" She trailed off her fingers going to her lips and then she stepped back from him and took his hand in hers, leading him back in the direction she'd come from.

"Where are you taking me?"

"Someplace where we can forget," she said, leading him closer to the Montez Denim tent where he could hear loud music blaring.

"What are you trying to forget?" he asked.

"That you were kissing me to distract yourself," she said. "I have no idea what you're running from. But dancing seems like it might be the solution."

Damn. He hated that she'd seen through him but knew it hadn't been that hard.

"Not here we won't. Come with me. I know a bar not that far away where we won't know everyone in the place. Then we can dance and forget and maybe for tonight I can remember that I'm young."

"We both are. Savanna says I act like I'm twenty-three going on forty."

He laughed. "Well…"

She mock punched him. "Hey. You're were supposed to say she was wrong."

"Was she?" he asked as they got to his truck. It was a big Chevy with four-wheel drive and a quad cab. His dad had insisted on going with him to the dealership to buy it.

He stopped rubbing his hand over his eyes as he felt that sting of tears. God, he was messed up. No amount of dancing and baring was going to cure that.

But then Sierra slipped her hand from his and pushed him back against the passenger door of his truck. She went up on her tiptoes, putting one hand against the side of his jaw, drawing his other arm down to her waist.

"Gage Powell, you're thinking way too much for this summer's night. Show me what it's like to be young and free."

Her lips brushed over his and for all the sweetness and innocence there was around her, there was a fire in her kiss that he didn't even try to resist. He lifted her off her feet and more fully into his body and let her soft curves drive his demons away.

SIERRA HAD A really long day. She'd been forced to face the fact that her father didn't really trust her when she'd noticed his assistant Bruce lurking around one of the other sponsor's booths at a fan event. She'd confronted Bruce who unfortunately for him hadn't picked up a bit of her father's backbone by working for the man for the last six months. And Sierra had been born with it. She'd lit into him and sent him scurrying back to Dallas.

She'd put off calling her father because she wasn't in the mood to hold her temper in check. And while letting it fly seemed like exactly what she wanted at this moment, she knew that letting him know he'd gotten the better of her would just let him believe he'd won. So instead she'd stomped away from the Montez Denim event and run smack into Gage.

He looked like he'd been running from something as well. She sure as heck figured he had a lot of demons but she wasn't interested in helping him fight them. She was interested in distraction. That was it.

She had been holding a candle burning at both ends with one hand while patting herself on the back with the other, telling herself she'd finally shown everyone at Montez Denim she was an adult and could do her damn job only to find out they'd been lying to her.

Or at least her dad had.

Hell.

She sighed.

"Darlin', that sigh was strong enough to be heard all the way down in Los Angeles. What's going on?"

"Nothing."

"Sure doesn't seem like nothing," he said.

"Listen, I thought you didn't do complicated. I thought you wanted a piece of tail and some bar hopping," she said still feeling ornery. "So, unless you've changed your mind leave it be."

"Damn, darlin', you seem like you want to fight. Are you sure you want to go there with me?"

She glanced over at him. Though it was nighttime he had his Stetson on and his features were illuminated by the dashboard lights so it wasn't hard for her to notice the twitch in his lips.

It just enflamed her temper. Another man acting like her anger was something cute and small and meant to be pooh-poohed instead of taking her seriously.

"Are you sure you do?" she asked. "Don't let my serious nature and buttoned-up appearance fool you. I spend a lot of my time biting my tongue and tonight I don't think I can do it."

He slowed the truck and signaled pulling onto the shoulder. They were on a stretch of highway that was deserted at this time of night and as he put the truck in park he reached over and turned the volume on the radio down to a low rumble of just bass and drums. He took off his seat belt before stretching one long arm along the back of the seat as he turned to face her.

"Let me have it."

Damn. He was being reasonable and one part of her—probably the sane bit—wanted to say forget it. But for the life of her it felt like she'd been a good girl and played by the rules for her entire life. And at this moment it felt like all of that had gotten her nowhere. There was no reward for being good except for disrespect and longing for what other people seemed to take for granted.

"Well for starters, Gage, I don't like being treated like my anger is something to be laughed at. I'm seriously ticked off right now."

He rested his other arm on the steering wheel and brought his hand over to cover his mouth.

"Hell, are you laughing at me again? I just can't deal with this tonight," she said, opening the door and hopping out of the cab. She landed hard on her feet, which sent a bit of pain shooting up her legs and that just spurred her to start walking. She had her cell phone in her back pocket and enough money on her platinum credit card to pay for transportation away from the dumbass redneck laughing his butt off at her expense.

"I'll show him. I've never in my days had to put up with such…ridiculous, douche baggy, pompous behavior and if I have to—"

She broke off her running monologue as she was jerked to a stop by Gage's arm around her waist. He lifted her off her feet, carried her under his arm like she didn't weigh more than his gear and walked back to the truck. He set her on the passenger seat where she'd left the door open and then just stood there. It bothered her a little that they were almost eye to eye. Damn he was tall.

"Now I'll be the first to admit that I was laughing but just because you are so damned cute," he began. "I'm not being a douche on purpose and Lord knows I'm pompous but you just made me smile when nothing else has for a long time. It wasn't at your expense; it stemmed from you."

She wasn't sure how that could be, but then he leaned in closer, putting his hands on her waist.

"I needed a distraction and I was looking for a fight and instead I found you. And you're doing the same thing so it puts me in mind of something that we could do to distract ourselves."

"Get laid," she said. He had to be thinking of a night of sex. Her mind was flooded with images of the two of them tangled together on the front seat in the cab of his truck. His long hard body on top of hers...

"Maybe... I'm not saying I don't want you, Sierra, but damn you are more than a piece of tail to me and I think we could both use a night of fun. You in?"

She'd already decided she was but then her own thoughts had led her to a dark and troubled place. "I'm game but you should know I'm not myself tonight."

"I haven't been myself in seven years so I guess we're even."

THE ROADSIDE BAR was the kind of dive that his momma had always warned him to stay away from. He was pretty sure that Sierra had never seen the inside of a place like this but she looked game.

She looked like he'd felt the first time he'd gotten on the back of a bull. He'd been twelve and determined to prove to his dad that he was as good as Marty. He'd puked his guts out behind the chute and then "manned up" and gotten on the bull rode for three seconds before being thrown.

Hell.

He'd forgotten how exhilarating that first ride had been. He'd popped to his feet feeling like he'd hung the moon. After all Marty hadn't made three seconds on his first ride. He'd looked around for his dad but he was nowhere to be seen. He'd been talking to one of the bull breeders about Marty's next ride and had missed Gage's debut.

He cursed under his breath.

"Are you okay?" she asked.

"Yeah. Nothing that some tequila shots and beer chasers won't cure. And maybe a dance with my best gal."

She winked at him. "Guess I'll have to do."

She opened the passenger door when he turned the engine off and he put his hand on her shoulder. "Wait for me. I'll help you down."

"Thanks," she said, glancing back at him, her hair brushing the back of his hand. He was sure he'd felt something softer and smoother in his life but in that moment, he couldn't recall what it had been.

He got out of the cab, pocketed his keys and walked around the truck to help her down. As soon as he set her on her feet, she stepped away from him. She wasn't putting up no-trespassing signs but she was definitely trying to put the brakes on whatever had been going on between them earlier. He'd been raised a gentleman so he'd respect whatever boundaries she set.

"Have you been here before?"

"No. But I have been to places like this all throughout the west. Hell, I've even been in some shady pubs in Scotland."

She stopped and shook her head. "Scotland? What were you doing there?"

"Dance with me and I'll tell you," he said.

"Buy me a drink and I'll dance with you," she retorted.

"Deal."

He opened the door for her and gestured for her to go in front of him. She took two steps inside and stopped. The music was loud. The dance floor was packed with gyrating couples some who didn't seem to notice they were in public. There was a haze in the air and it smelled of smoke even though it had been years since anyone could light up in the bar and the smell of alcohol seemed to permeate every surface.

He breathed it in. This was what he needed.

He glanced at Sierra. She looked like she was seconds away from bolting. He grabbed her by the waist and swung her into his arms as the jukebox started to play "Redneck Woman" by Gretchen Wilson. It was an oldie that he remembered from the nights of drinking and fighting after

Marty's death.

She put her hand on his chest and he danced with her, keeping her close. He'd told himself he was doing this for her. That he was trying to be her hero. But the truth was he needed it. He couldn't go back to the trailer and his thoughts. To the sad, pitiful thoughts that waited for him there as he tried to make sense of why he was striving so damned hard to be the son his father wanted when his dad would never be the parent that Gage wanted him to be.

"I thought…"

He pulled her close and leaned down so he could talk into her ear. "Don't think. Thinking is why we were both running tonight. Just feel."

She put her hands on his waist and held on to him like he did when he got on the back of a bull. And he wanted to tell her there was no way he was going to try to buck her off, but talking wasn't really where he shone. He knew that, so instead he pulled her close and danced with her until the music changed. They danced until he was hot and sweaty and wanted more than a drink; but there was a hint of vulnerability in Sierra's eyes. He glanced around for a table and found one near the back of the bar by the pool tables and he led her away from the dance floor toward the table.

He signaled the waitress and realized that he probably shouldn't get too smashed if he was going to drive later but he also knew he could handle a couple of beers and maybe a shot of tequila. So he ordered two shots, two beers and then settled back in the booth across from Sierra.

"It's time for you to pay up, cowboy," she said, as the drinks arrived.

She licked the back of her hand, shook a little salt on it and then downed her tequila like a pro. His jeans got a little tighter, proving that not touching her wasn't the key to cooling down.

"What'd you have in mind, darlin'?" he asked downing his shot.

She skimmed her gaze down his body, lingering on his chest, before looking at his mouth again. She leaned over and the front of her blouse gaped from her skin, revealing the barest hint of her cleavage. He groaned and shifted his legs under the table.

"You owe me a story," she said, with a wink, picking up the lime he'd left on the table next to his empty shot glass. She lifted it to her mouth and licked the juice from the wedge.

Chapter Three

A SLIGHT BIT of stubble darkened his jaw and Sierra knew she'd probably had enough to drink because she wanted to rest her elbow on the table and put her chin on her hand and stare at him. The sixteen-year-old inside of her couldn't believe she was sitting across from Gage in a bar. This was crazy.

But so perfect.

The anger and upset she'd experienced earlier seemed a long time away and she was glad to finally distance herself from it. He smiled at her as the waitress dropped off two more shots of tequila and she reached for hers and downed it. He arched one eyebrow at her before doing the same.

"Okay, cowboy, talk."

"Technically I'm not a cowboy."

"You're not? You sure as heck look like one," she said.

"I'll give you that. So, what did you want to know?" he asked, a grin teasing the sides of his mouth.

He was flirting with her and she couldn't help that crazy, giddy feeling that grew in the pit of her stomach. "Scotland. I want to know how you ended up there."

"Where did you think I'd been?" he asked.

"I don't know. I heard rumors that you'd gone down south to ride," she said. "Like Kane."

"Nah. I went south to the Gulf and got a job working on an oil rig."

"What? That's crazy," she said. "Did you miss bull riding?"

"Sometimes but after Marty…well I just walked away. And the oil rig was a good place to go. No one at the company knew who I was except some young Okie. And that suited me just fine."

"So how did you end up in Scotland?" she asked. She wanted to know more about walking away from bull riding but his voice had gotten tense and even in her feel-good state she knew he didn't want to talk about it.

"Got a promotion," he said, taking a swallow of his beer. She watched his throat work as he swallowed.

His throat was long and strong. He had a strong jaw too. Not weak like Bruce who'd asked her out a few times. She'd said no because she'd been pretty sure he'd asked because he wanted to advance his career at Montez Denim. Gage wouldn't skulk around spying on someone. "You're staring at me."

"I like the way you look," she said.

"I'm glad you do."

"I know," she said. She wondered if this euphoria was what Savanna felt. If this was why she'd spent all her time moving from one new relationship to another. It was nice to feel like this without the pressure of trying to make something work. Maybe…

"Good. Do you know I want to kiss you?"

She leaned in closer to him. "I suspected as much."

"Did I answer all of your questions?"

"Nope," she said. "Why?"

He snagged her hand in his, drawing her arm forward the slightest bit and rubbing his thumb over the back of her knuckles. "I was hoping to get you back on the dance floor. Maybe play a slow song on the jukebox and make you forget about oil rigs, sponsors and this place."

She turned her hand under his, lacing their fingers together. His hands were rough. Working man's hands, she thought. There were cuts and callouses on them and she rubbed her finger over them. Saw the way her pretty Summer Berry manicured nails looked against his tanned hands and imagined them on her body.

She wanted him.

She'd spent a lot of time working her ass off and focusing on her career, pretending that bull riders weren't her cup of tea—especially this one; but he was exactly what she wanted.

"I wouldn't mind a slow dance."

"Then ask your questions, darlin', because once I take you in my arms again I'm not going to be thinking about talking."

A pulse of liquid heat went through her and she felt that

emptiness between her legs. She wasn't thinking about anything beyond this booth. Beyond his hand in hers and how good he'd felt earlier when they'd been dancing and how she'd wished she'd opened her legs when he'd lifted her onto the seat of his truck and drawn him closer to her.

But she hadn't felt brave then. Not like she did now.

She hadn't felt like the kind of woman who could reach out and take what she needed.

"Why Scotland?" she asked. It was the one question she had and then she was ready to forget about getting to know him better through conversation.

"It was as far away from Oklahoma as I could get," he said.

He didn't strike her as a man who'd run away from anything. But watching his brother die…that had to have cut through him in a way that nothing else could have. She saw those stormy shadows darken his expression. He was forgetting the fun and the flirtation.

"Okay, that's it. Let's dance," she said, sliding out of the booth, and he hesitated.

She slipped onto the bench next to him, scooted over and put her forehead against his. Their faces were so close she could feel the brush of his breath against her lips each time he exhaled and see the tiny flecks of blue in his gray eyes. "We're young. Remember? Tonight is about living in the moment. Forget the past and whatever drove you to Scotland. That's not what we both want tonight."

"No, it's not," he said, tugging her off balance.

She fell sideways into his arms and across his lap. He held her to him with his arm around her waist and caught a strand of her hair with his other hand. Rubbed it between his fingers before he lowered his head and took her mouth in a kiss that tasted of tequila and passion. Of unanswered questions and burning desires.

THE PLACE HAD an energy that made it impossible for her to hang on to the vestiges of the anger she'd felt toward her father. Though she had to admit a big part of that was generated from Gage. He had left his Stetson on the table and if she thought it strange that he could dance as well as he could, well… Why could he?

She leaned in close. His hand accidentally brushed her breast and he smiled at her and winked. She flushed. She felt the heat on her cheeks and her chest. She really needed to get over her reaction to him, but a part of her liked it.

"How come you can dance so well?" she asked.

"I like girls. Girls like to dance. So I had to learn how to do it well," he said.

She liked his logic. There was a part of him that seemed pretty straightforward, though she knew he was hiding something too. He only let her get so close and some of his answers were meant to make her think of him in a certain context.

Good ol' boy.

Except her daddy was a good ol' boy as were all her uncles, so she wasn't buying Gage's show. Not all of it. She thought probably part of him was just what he seemed.

A country waltz came on, "Neon Moon", an old tune by Brooks & Dunn. He grabbed her hand and pulled her into his arms. She looked up into his face, saw that his eyes weren't serious and whatever demons had been riding him earlier seemed to have retreated. He watched her like…well, like she was the most important woman in the world to him. As if the world had narrowed to just the two of them and they were all that mattered.

And this was Gage who she'd been half in love with since she was sixteen. She wanted to believe what she saw in his eyes was real, but she prided herself on being realistic. And he hadn't really even known she existed until tonight.

She couldn't shut out the rest of it. The couple that were wrapped around each other like they'd been superglued that way, their mouths fused. The drunk guy behind her who kept bumping into her as he tried to swing his girl to the music. The jukebox that sometimes got loud for a second and then balanced back to normal.

"How do you do that?" she asked. "How do you concentrate on just one thing?"

He shrugged. "It's a skill I developed for riding. You have to be able to shut out everything and focus on the ride.

If you don't, you end up dead. And I don't want to die."

Spontaneously she hugged him. "I don't want that either."

"Thanks," he said. "I know…"

He trailed off and she didn't have to ask. He'd seen his brother gored by a bull and watched him die. No one should have to face that as frequently as she was pretty sure Gage did. Probably each time he got on a bull.

"So, I'm guessing your focus is only for the few seconds you need to win the gold belt."

"Don't worry, darlin', I've got staying power."

She blushed again. Okay, seriously, this had to stop. "I wasn't asking about that."

"Weren't you?" he teased. His hands drifted down to her hips and he pulled her closer to him. She noticed he fit nicely against her. Her head naturally fell to his shoulder and his arms held her close as he swung her around to the music and away from the drunk.

She closed her eyes and realized he was singing under his breath. About being beneath a neon moon. It was a bit of a sad song. She wondered if he thought of them that way.

It was a tale of broken love and she guessed it was a warning she should heed. There wasn't a single Montez who had figured out how to make a relationship last and there was a sweetness to Gage that she hadn't seen before. She'd been so busy taking in his muscled frame and the way his butt looked in classic Montez Denim button-flies that she hadn't let herself dwell on the fact that he might need someone who could listen to him. The kind of gal who'd help him get over the death of his brother and whatever the fallout from that was that had sent him on the run.

Could she do that?

She wasn't too sure. She had her career and it was finally starting to move to a place where she wanted it to go. She wasn't like Savanna who liked having a guy in her bed every night—seriously her sister had said that one time.

But when Gage held her close, swaying to the fiddle and electric guitar and singing under his breath, she wanted to grab his hand and run away. Run far away from the AEBR Tour and Montez Denim and his past and her present.

Just go someplace where nothing existed but the two of them.

And how childish was that? she wondered.

Running away wasn't the way to deal with this. She liked him. Not just his rock-hard abs and tight ass. She liked his crooked smile and the way he teased her and called her darlin'. She finally understood something that she'd thought she'd gotten all along. That attraction didn't follow any rules she'd made up for herself. In theory, she should be able to just have sex with him and walk away.

Hook up and be all casual about it later; but she knew she wasn't going to be able to do that. She wasn't ever going to forget that moment when the music stopped playing and she looked up into those gray eyes of his and realized that he meant more to her than she'd thought he would.

That her long ago crush had been nothing compared to the feelings welling up in her now. She wanted to say something so that he'd know this wasn't casual to her. But then she thought it might be to him.

Just because she liked him didn't mean he felt the same. She might just be his Sacramento hookup.

SIERRA FELT RIGHT in his arms. Her lips moved under his, her tongue rubbing over his and her mouth opening as she tipped her head to the side to deepen the kiss. He twirled a strand of her hair around his finger and then pushed his hand into her hair, cupping the back of her head. She moaned deep in her throat and he realized he'd had enough of the bar. Maybe he'd never really wanted to come here at all.

Sierra was the only thing he needed for what was on his mind. Fighting seemed a pale way to get rid of the demons riding him when faced with her sweet curves. Sierra tamed something wild inside of him that he'd never realized was howling to get out until now. Until her.

He took her hand in his and led her off the dance floor and over to the booth where he'd stashed his hat.

"Do you want another drink?"

She shook her head. "I think I've had enough of the bar."

"Me too."

He took her hand and walked out of the bar with the intent of getting to his truck. As soon as he stepped outside the night air wrapped around him, reminding him it was late summer. She laughed as she stumbled against him, throwing her head back and staring up at the night sky.

"What? You don't want to dance anymore?"

He lifted her off her feet, pulling her into his arms. "Would you rather dance in there?"

"Nope," she said, wrapping her legs around his waist and her arms around his shoulders. "No man has ever carried me before and you've done it twice tonight."

"You're just a tiny thing," he said.

"Which doesn't explain why you keep picking me up," she said. "Not complaining by the way. I like the way your biceps bulge each time you do it."

He couldn't explain it without feeling super foolish so he kept his mouth shut. "You like my arms?"

"I do. But honestly, Gage, there isn't much on you I don't like," she said, sighing a little. "I've always felt so superior to Savanna and my momma but tonight I finally get it. I can see how they lose their heads over a man."

"Is that what you're doing?" he asked. He had forgotten he might be a novelty to her. That he might be her bull rider just like Savanna had set her sights on one of the Brazilian riders.

"Well I'm not thinking like myself. But you know what?

I've been playing by the rules all my life and no one takes me seriously. No matter what I do…for once I want to take what I want. Not think about the consequences. Just live in the moment."

"Like you told me to do," he said, walking with her in his arms toward the truck. When he got to his pickup truck he heard the doors unlock with the proximity alert he'd set up when he got his new ride. He held her easily with one arm and opened the door, setting her down on the seat.

This time she kept her arms around him. She leaned down to kiss him and knocked his hat askew, then she took it off his head and tossed it onto the back seat of his quad cab. She put her hands on either side of his head, tunneling her fingers through his hair. She tipped his head back and he looked up at her. Saw the longing and desire that echoed the same feelings deep in his soul.

"Darlin', you're making me think things…"

"What things?"

"Stuff that I haven't really had a thought about in a long time. Things that could distract me from what's important," he admitted.

"What is it?" she asked. "Whatever it is, you can tell me."

He believed that he could. But he didn't want to share the complicated relationship he had with his parents. How his mom was both afraid for him and proud of him for being the bigger man. How his dad was treating him in a way that Gage had never really believed the old man could. How every day he got a little deeper into needing to win not for himself, not for the joy of riding but because that was the only way he could convince himself to keep the lie going.

And somehow when he held Sierra, even though he barely knew her, she made him feel like maybe winning wasn't the be-all and end-all. He really hoped to hell that feeling was wrong because he knew he was broken. And a complicated mess. And it was one thing to kiss her and take her on the front seat of his truck. But something else entirely if he got attached to her.

He had never been able to make anyone stay when he wanted them to. Never really tried because he'd always known there was something broken inside of him. Something that was destructive and hurtful—

"Gage, stop. Whatever it is you're thinking just stop. Tonight, I'm not your sponsor and you're not one of our riders. Tonight, we're just Sierra and Gage and neither of us have to worry about the future. This is it. Just tonight."

Tonight.

She was saying the right things. That was exactly the kind of woman he wanted and needed. And if he could just convince his mind that this wasn't a mistake.

But then she wrapped those long legs of hers around him and pulled him closer with her fingers wrapped around the back of his neck. She arched her back as she drew his head down to hers and this time when their mouths met they weren't in the parking lot of a bar. There was only him and her and the bed of his truck and the night sky filled with stars and a waning moon to see them.

And that was all he needed. He shifted her in his arms, took control of the kiss and stopped looking for reasons to walk away when all he really wanted tonight was her.

Chapter Four

S HE WISHED SHE'D worn a skirt or something that he could slide his hands up underneath so she could feel his hands on her skin instead of on the fabric of her jeans. But she'd been working today and Montez Denim was her life and her job.

He put his large hands on her waist, pulling her forward to the edge of the seat until he was standing right between her legs. She felt his abdomen pressing against her and it wasn't enough. She had that empty ache deep inside of her and she needed more of him. She arched her back and his mouth slid from hers, nibbling down the edge of her jaw to the line of her neck.

He kissed his way down to her collarbone where her blousy shirt fell toward the edge of her shoulders, leaving an expanse of skin bare to him. Her hair fell around her shoulders.

"It's better like this."

"What is?" she asked. Honestly nothing felt better. He felt good and he made her ache in the most delicious way but she doubted she was going to be better until he was buried deep inside of her.

"Your hair. Damn, it's pretty. I keep thinking it's brown but there is so much more color to it than that."

"I have it colored," she said. She did it so she didn't look as much like Savanna and their mom, who had deep ebony-colored hair.

He chuckled and she realized how ridiculous it was to tell him that.

"Well I like it," he said at last. "You've got two choices, darlin'."

She loved the way he called her darlin' all long and slow. It made her feel all warm and drippy like honey.

"Yes," she said, but the word was raspy and not very solid.

He rubbed his thumb over her bottom lip and her nipples hardened. She wasn't sure how much more of this teasing she could take before she just reached into his jeans and took what she wanted from him. She didn't know if it was his intent to tease her or if he was trying to do the cowboy thing. Being all gentlemanly. But she was almost to her breaking point.

"We can do this here and now or we could go back to your place and take our time on the bed," he said.

She realized that she was about to have a night with the man she'd spent the better part of seven years fantasizing about. And being timid or shy wasn't in the cards. Knowing her own track record with men, she figured she better do everything she could tonight. Because she might not get another chance with him.

She shifted back to put a little space between their bodies and ran her finger down the center of his neck over the leather necklace that held a small medallion. She looked up at him from under her lashes.

"I think you forgot an option."

"Did I?" he asked.

She nodded. "Both."

"Both works for me."

She thought it would. She'd never been risky or bold. Not really. She thought she was sometimes because who wanted to think of themselves as a wimp? But the reality was there had seldom been anything she wanted enough to take a chance on. Something she'd never realized until tonight this moment when Gage was standing between her spread thighs looking like temptation. Tonight she was tired of always being the "smart" sister. She wanted to be swept away by the passion he easily called from her.

"I thought it would," she said.

He drew her closer again. His hands tightened on her, drawing her off the seat until her feet touched the ground. He let her slide down the front of his body, each of her curves gliding over the muscly hardness of him. She had always lusted over muscled men when she saw the bull riders they sponsored but until this moment hadn't appreciated the hardness of a male frame pressed against hers.

She sighed.

Damn.

He laughed. The demons that had been dogging him all night seemed to have fled and she realized that fighting would have definitely gotten rid of the adrenaline that had been riding her, but sex was a much better way to do it.

He tangled his hands in her hair, drawing his fingers through it from her scalp and letting the strands fall to her shoulders. Her hair wasn't long and certainly she never really thought of the thick mass as anything other than a pain to style, but the way he fondled her hair made her realize he liked it.

She tipped her head back, looking up at him in the shadowy light of the parking lot and noticed that she could see his expression better now than she could under the brim of his Stetson. His hair was thick and short. She ran her fingers through it and despite the fact that it had been flattened by the hat it was springy and soft under her fingers.

"What are you doing?" he asked, his voice a deep raspy growl.

"Just seeing if your hair feels good under my fingers," she said, running her hands over his scalp, scraping her nail around his ear and down his neck. He shivered as he tightened one hand in her hair and drew her head back, bringing his mouth down hard on hers. This time there was no seduction in his kiss, just a raw aching need that left her hungry for more.

He thrust his tongue deep into her mouth and she sucked hard on it, answering his thrust with one of her own. She was pulled deeper into the swirling whirlpool of desire. Her blood felt hotter in her veins. Her skin suddenly was sensitive to everything and her clothing was too restrictive. She needed to be naked. She wanted him naked.

She needed his body pressed against hers and she wanted it now.

GAGE HAD STOPPED thinking. Stopped worrying about if he should take her, knowing he was going to. He'd spent most of his life running and denying he wanted or needed anything but tonight he knew he needed Sierra.

She had calmed something wild inside of him and awakened this…he didn't have a word to describe it since he'd never experienced it before. He only knew that he wasn't going to walk away from her.

She wanted him too. Her eyes watched him with a rapt attention that made him want to stand taller and stick out his chest. Made him want to grab her, mark her and claim her as his. Her mouth moved under his with passion and desire, fanning the already out of control blaze in his veins. He had pulled out of the truck because he couldn't get close enough to her, but now as she skimmed her hands down the front of his chest, undoing the buttons of his western-cut shirt as she went, he wondered if that had been a mistake.

He ran his hands up and down her back before drawing her closer to him, grinding his erection against the notch at the top of her thighs and she groaned as her head fell to the side, exposing her neck and thrusting her breasts forward. He buried his face between her breasts using his teeth to pull the elastic at the top of her blouse lower. He brought his hand up and drew the neckline of her peasant top down until it was tucked under her bra. She wore a nude fabric bra that did nothing to hide her taut nipples.

He felt a pulse of liquid desire between his legs and realized it had been a long time since a woman had gotten him this hot. He tongued her nipple through the fabric of her bra and then scraped his teeth gently over it.

She arched again, wrapping one thigh around his hips and rubbing against his erection. He wanted to take this slow but knew that the parking lot wasn't the place for that. Besides there was always later. He figured it was going to take him at least until morning to sate the hunger he had for her.

He found the button fastening of her jeans and undid it before lowering the zipper and sliding his hand inside her pants. He felt her warmth against his fingers as he cupped her intimately. She scored her nails down his chest, her fingers scraping over his hard nipples in a sensation he wasn't too sure he liked but then she moved lower.

He used his free hand to undo her bra and then nudged

the fabric out of his way with his nose as he took her nipple into his mouth, suckling on her as his fingers explored between her legs.

She rocked her hips forward as he touched her, tapping lightly on her, and she moaned. Her own hand was stroking him through the fabric of his jeans and making him strain against the denim.

She undid the buttons of his jeans, her mouth on his throat. Kissing and licking against him, whispering something too soft for him to understand. Then she shifted and bit the lobe of his ear as her hand slipped into the opening of his jeans and under the band of his underwear to encircle his length. Her hand was cool and soft against him. He thrust up into her grip and she tightened it, running her hand up and down his shaft.

He felt that tingling down his back and knew he was getting close to the edge. He grabbed her wrist and pulled her hand from his pants. She started to object but he caught her mouth under his and thrust his tongue deep into her mouth, to keep her from talking. She used both hands to shove her panties and jeans down her legs below her knees and he lifted her up onto the seat of his truck again.

She sat there, her hair tousled, her lips swollen, her eyes watching him with a hunger he knew he could sate.

He took her shoes off and pulled her jeans down her legs and tossed them on the floor of the truck before removing her panties and tucking them into his back pocket. She wrapped her arms around his shoulders as he cupped her naked backside in his hands, running his finger lightly between her cheeks.

She arched her back, as he caught her nipple in his mouth and suckled it. He turned his attention to her other nipple when he was done and she started to arch against him. He put his hands on the top of her thighs, running his fingers along the inside all the way up to her center. He lifted his mouth from her body and stepped back to look at her. His hands were on her thighs, her breasts were exposed and her secrets were there for the taking. He palmed her body and thrust the tip of one finger inside her, drawing out the wet tip and bringing it to his mouth and licking it.

"You taste good, darlin'."

She just groaned as he parted her and leaned down to tongue the tiny little bud between her legs. He flicked his tongue over it as her hands tightened in his hair. He entered her again with one finger and as she thrust up he continued to eat her intimate flesh so delicately. Her thighs tightened around his head and he added a second finger in her body, shoving them both in and out of her as her body tightened around him.

Her hands clasped his head to her body as she cried out his name and thrust her hips urgently against his mouth. Then she arched her back and collapsed against the seat as the storm inside of her raged on. He lifted his head and looked up at her. Saw the flush of passion on her skin and tasted her in his mouth. He watched her as she stared down at him for a minute and knew that walking away from her was going to be harder than he wanted to admit.

HER BODY WAS still buzzing and pulsing, but she wanted more. She needed him between her legs and not just a few fingers. She didn't think beyond getting him where she wanted him. She scooted back on the seat, beckoning him up inside the cab of the truck with one finger.

He climbed up onto the passenger seat and shut the door behind him.

"Do you have a condom?" she asked. "I'm on the pill, but…"

"Don't worry, darlin', I've got it covered," he said, reaching for the glove box and pulling out a box of condoms.

Another time it might bother her that he carried a box in his truck but right now she was just glad that it meant she didn't have to wait to have him inside of her. He opened the pack and put the condom on and she crawled over to him and straddled his lap. She shifted on him, felt him at the entrance of her body before she sank down on him, taking him completely inside of her. She felt his hands on her butt holding her in place when she wanted to move.

He arched his back and went even deeper and she groaned. He was so thick and hard and filled her completely.

She tipped her head back, felt her own hair brushing on her shoulders, and then opened her eyes to see he was watching her. He tangled his hands in her hair again and she realized he wasn't holding her still so she started to move on him. Lifting herself until only the tip of him remained inside of her and then shifting back down until he filled her again. She put her hands on his shoulders and rode him hard. Up and down until she felt the climax building inside of her again.

He lowered his head, his mouth on her left breast suckling her while he kept one hand in her hair and the other on her hips urging her to move faster, to take him deeper. She kept rocking against him until she felt her orgasm burst through her. She cried out his name and he wrapped both arms around her, thrusting up inside of her and going faster and faster until his entire body shuddered underneath hers and he groaned her name.

She wrapped her arms around him as he rested his head against her breast and she just held him. He held her too, both of them clinging to each other. The storm of passion had forced them here to this spot and all of the other things that had been on her mind faded away.

He held her so tightly to him.

And all she could think about was Gage.

He rubbed his hands up and down her back and she rested her head on his shoulder. Not thinking about anything but him. For once she didn't have that anxious knot in the pit of her stomach.

"I guess we should think about leaving the parking lot,"

he said.

"Are you coming back to my hotel?" she asked.

"Unless you've changed your mind," he said. He ran his hands up her back as she shifted back on his thighs, pulling their bodies apart.

"I haven't," she said.

He lifted her off his lap and set her on the seat next to him. They both put their clothing back on and he pulled her panties from his back pocket and handed them to her. She had to laugh and soon he started laughing too. It was such an awkward but not sweet moment as they were both bumping into each other as she struggled to get back into her jeans.

When they were both dressed again, he got out and walked around to the driver's side of the truck and she watched him. The way he moved got to her. He walked with the confidence of a man who knew his place in the world and when he opened the door and climbed behind the wheel, glancing over at her, she knew she should stop staring but didn't.

"What?"

"I just like the way you move."

"Really? Well," he said, wriggling his brows at her, "I've got a few more moves to show you. Where are you staying?"

She told him and put on her seat belt as he started the engine. He put on a local country music station that was playing oldies that she remembered her mom listening to when she'd been growing up. She tipped her head back against the seat and finally realized that she knew why

Savanna was always looking for this connection with a guy. It made sense to her now.

"What are you thinking?"

"Nothing I want to say out loud."

"Fair enough. How'd you like your first dive bar?" he asked as the miles passed.

She thought about it for a long while. She wouldn't have said she liked the place but being anywhere with Gage was certainly enough to make her want to go back again.

"It was different. The company was great."

"Yeah?"

She nodded. She wanted to ask him if he had enjoyed the night with her, but didn't want to be that vulnerable. She knew in that instant that sex hadn't really solved everything the way it had felt like it had when they'd finished. Now she realized that she wanted more from him and she wasn't sure he wanted anything from her.

Why hadn't she thought of that before?

He pulled up to the reception area at her hotel and looked over at her.

"Second thoughts?"

Yes.

Hell yes.

But letting him walk away tonight wasn't what she wanted. Tomorrow would be soon enough to find out what the future had in store for her where this man was concerned. Tonight, she wanted everything he had to give.

Chapter Five

G AGE FOLLOWED HER through the lobby of the luxury hotel she'd booked. Sacramento was one of the bigger towns on the tour and if he'd forgotten that he and Sierra were from two different worlds that point was driven home to him as the concierge greeted her by name and asked if she needed anything sent up to her room.

"Thank you, Henry," she said. "I'm hungry. What about you?"

She turned to Gage with a sparkle in her eye and he noticed that her lips were still a bit swollen from his kisses and that she had a bit of stubble burn on her neck. He needed to shave. Surely a posh place like this one would have a razor in the bathroom.

"I seem to have worked up an appetite," he said.

"Me too! Henry, we'll have two cheeseburgers and fries, and I want a chocolate shake. Gage?"

"Strawberry shake for me," he said. He liked that she wasn't ordering something healthy even though it was almost midnight... Hell, a smart man who wanted to stay in the money would be calling it a night.

But no one had ever raved about his intelligence. His stubbornness and his determination, sure. But not his smarts.

"I'll have them sent up. Anything else?" Henry asked.

"A razor," Gage said. "I need to shave."

Henry nodded and then Sierra took his hand in hers and led him toward the bank of elevators. The floor was some kind of swanky hard marble and the heels of his fancy Kelly boots echoed as he followed her.

While they waited for the elevator car to come, she kept his hand in hers. Like they were a couple.

A real couple.

Like he belonged to her and she belonged to him.

And for a man who'd been wandering as long as he had, that was scary. He was a loner by nature and circumstance but Sierra wasn't.

She thought… Hell what he wanted was what she thought. That maybe this could be the start of something. But he was a man who was trying to earn his father's respect even if that meant letting him believe he was his brother. Gage had made his peace with it.

But he doubted that anyone else would understand. He knew that he had to keep winning to keep in his dad's good graces…and here he was with Sierra.

Holding her hand and then when they stepped into the empty elevator car, he contemplated kissing her.

Hell he wanted more than a kiss. Sex in his truck had simply whetted his appetite for her and like a starving man offered a free meal he wasn't going to worry about how to pay the bill later.

Tomorrow was soon enough.

He wrapped his arm around her and held her close to his side. She smelled faintly of whiskey from the bar he'd taken her to and of sex.

Which made his body respond. He still wanted her. Once wasn't enough. He was pretty sure that one hundred times wasn't going to be enough for him.

The door opened on her floor and she led the way down the hall to her suite. She opened the door and he looked around the large entryway with a sitting area and small kitchenette and then there was a closed door that he assumed led to the bathroom.

"Do you want the grand tour?"

"Sure. I think I could use a shower," he said. "I'm sure a fancy place like this has robes in the room."

She tipped her head to the side. "They do. Does it bother you that this is where I'm staying?"

"In what way?" he asked.

She shrugged. "You know my family has money."

"I do."

"It makes some men...well, just behave oddly. That's all," she said.

She must get her fair share of gold diggers looking for an easy ride. But he'd never been one to ride on someone else's coat tails, preferring to make his own way. "That's not what

I meant. Just that I want to wash the smell of the roadside bar off of me before I climb into bed with you."

She blushed, which he had to admit he found enchanting. He'd seen her in her corporate, professional mode and she was beyond competent in the way she worked. He knew the entire rookie campaign that Montez Denim was running this year had been her brainchild. She was smart as a whip and confident in every part of her life but with him she was shy.

Was it just him or all men?

That wasn't a question he wanted to ask or contemplate.

"Since you put it that way I could probably use a shower too," she said. "Let me show you the bathroom. There's one of those huge rain showers and a garden tub."

He followed her through the living area and into the bedroom, which was dominated by a king-sized bed. She flicked on the lights as she continued to the bathroom and he followed her.

"This place feels huge. And it's not just because I've been living in the camper while I'm on tour. My bunk on the oil rig was tiny as well."

"I want to know more about that," she said. "I can't imagine working and living in the same place."

"You do though, don't you?" he asked. "Montez Denim is based in Dallas and you live there."

"True but there are about a million other people who live there too," she said. "I know that's not an accurate population count but you know what I mean. And I drive to work out of my little neighborhood. I mean it's a lot different than being contained in one location. I guess what I meant is how don't you go stir-crazy?"

"Fair enough," he said. "I wasn't going to correct you on the population."

She shook her head. "Sorry, that was habit. My dad likes accurate statistics. And I'm more of a generalist. So, he's always like: were there really a million people in front of you at Starbucks this morning…ugh, right?"

He laughed as he realized her shyness earlier was just nerves. Now that he was in the suite and they were talking she was starting to settle down. Which was exactly what he wanted. This night might be their only one together and he wanted to make it one that she'd never forget.

SIERRA AND GAGE were sitting in front of the TV watching an old movie that he hadn't seen since he'd been working on the oil rig when it came out. It was one of those superhero ones where they all band together to save the earth.

"I'm going to have to go to the gym tomorrow but this cheeseburger was exactly what I needed," she said. They'd both showered and he'd shaved. She'd offered to send his clothes down to be laundered so they'd be clean for the morning, but he'd declined. They were both wearing the hotel robes.

"Why were you so…out of sorts this evening?" he asked. "I think it had something to do with your dad."

"Yeah," she said, taking her time chewing the bite of burger she had in her mouth. She wiped her lips before turning to him. Normally she wouldn't have said anything to him about Montez Denim because he worked for the company.

"He sent his assistant to check up on me," she said. "It's not enough for the board that I've managed to increase our market share since the start of the campaign and I have to tell you that the AEBR fans are really responding to the posters and the fan events."

"I can tell. In the first few cities we were getting a small amount of fans but you saw how it was today. They're lining up and waiting for us all. It's not just like that for me," he said. "I think it helps that we're winning."

"It does help. I didn't mean in any way to take away from your skill, but the campaign was my idea and I had to fight with the board to convince them I could run it."

"Why?" he asked. "I can understand it from your father's perspective but what about the rest of the board."

"We're a family-held company so everyone on the board is related to me or married to someone related to me. They all remember when I had braces or when I worked summers in high school and they still see me as that teenager instead of a professional."

She realized she was one step away from whining and stopped. "Anyway, Dad is the absolute worst and when I saw Bruce skulking around today I lit into him and told him to go back to Dallas. I don't need him there watching me."

"You certainly don't," he said.

"Thanks. So what about you? You were...running like there was a rogue bull behind you and no rodeo clown to distract it."

He leaned back, stretching his arms along the back of the couch. He'd shaved and he looked younger without the stubble, with a hint of vulnerability that she normally wouldn't associate with him.

"It's complicated."

"If you don't want to say that's fine," she said, feeling like he probably didn't want to talk to her because—well, the only thing she could think of was that he must see her as a hookup. Someone he was getting busy with but not someone he wanted to share the details of his life with.

"It's not that. It involves my family. My dad has Alzheimer's and some days he's really lucid and he seems normal. He does the ranch chores and talks with the hands like his old self and then the next day he's talking about stuff that makes no sense to my mom."

"Oh, Gage. That's got to be so hard. I'm sorry. I shouldn't have said what I did." She really wasn't good at this sort of thing. What could she say? It sucked. She had been lucky in that no one close to her had anything seriously wrong with them, health wise.

"It's okay. I haven't really talked about it. It's not something that I bring up when I'm out drinking with the guys."

"I hope I didn't push you into sharing more than you wanted to," she said.

"No, you didn't. Tonight while I was sitting in my trailer watching the playback from the qualifying and thinking about my ride, he called and he wasn't himself. It just sort of set me off."

She could see that. Whether he admitted it or not, she guessed it had to be hard for him to be on tour. The memories of his brother had to be stronger here than they were on the oil rig. Which he admitted wasn't a place that had given him a lot of time to think about anything other than the job most days.

"Wish you were back on the North Sea?"

"Some days…yeah, I do. It was easier there. No one knew about Marty; my dad never called me. But then if I was out there I wouldn't be here with you."

That made her feel like more than a hookup. But he was a charming guy. She liked it when he called her darlin' with that sweet accent of his but a part of her wondered if he did that because he didn't know or couldn't remember her name. Which made her feel a little less than special.

She wondered how Savanna did this. She was always starting something new every two or three weeks. Was that what she liked? The getting to know each other but only sharing what you wanted?

Because she realized that while she told him about her dad, she hadn't told him about how she wanted to be different than her sister and her mom. How she wanted her dad's respect and wanted everyone to see her as Sierra not Davis's daughter.

Which made her realize that Gage had to be telling her only part of what had really been going on earlier tonight. She believed it had something to do with his dad and his Alzheimer's but what else was there?

And was it really any of her business?

Tonight, it wasn't.

She looked back at the screen. "This is the best part. Wait until you see the way they all come together to fight. I love it. They are all these big egos and damaged souls but when the chips are down they just do what needs to be done."

She noticed he was staring at her.

"Doing what needs to be done is important to you, isn't it?"

"I think it's important to everyone," she said. "Otherwise…well, nothing could ever be completed."

"I know. No matter how onerous the task is, once I start something I have to finish it."

He didn't say anything else until the movie was over but she'd been unable to concentrate on the screen when she had Gage sitting so close to her, making her wonder about the task he had to finish.

TALKING ABOUT HIS dad always made him edgy and a little angry. The movie was distracting but not enough for him to realize that if Sierra knew the truth she'd…well who really knew what she'd do. But if he heard of someone doing what he was doing, Gage knew he'd think the guy was a loser.

He sighed.

"What?"

"Nothing. Just thinking about how at twenty-five I'm still fighting old insecurities when it comes to my dad," he said.

She turned to face him on the couch, curling her legs up under her body. "Me too. Don't laugh but I thought once I turned twenty-one everything was going to magically get better. Like Dad would see me as an adult. Mom would stop trying to make me wear clothes and makeup I didn't want to, you know?"

"I do. So what kind of clothes does your mom want you to wear?" he asked seizing the distraction. He liked the way Sierra looked in anything, he realized. Even the oversized robe with the sleeves rolled up to her wrists.

"Do you know what Junior League is?" Sierra asked.

"Nope. Not a clue."

"Thank your lucky stars," she said, with a wink. "I'm

joking. They are a service organization for society woman. I really love the charity part of it but they do have…well according to mom, standards that should be maintained at all times. And a lady should always look like a lady."

"That doesn't sound so bad."

"Well I can sort of see why you'd say that but imagine dressing like a forty-year-old? I mean dresses and pearls and I don't mind being a little preppy but twenty-four/seven? No way. I really just like to be me."

"And your mom doesn't get it?" he asked. That sounded so much like his relationship with his father.

"She gets it. She doesn't approve," Sierra said. "Last time I came back from out of town, she'd purchased an entirely new wardrobe for me and had her housekeeper come over to my house and organize it for me in my closet."

"That's crazy."

"I know. Please tell me I'm not alone in this," she said.

"No one is concerned with what I wear except for you," he said. "Apparently you like me in skintight jeans and no shirt."

She blushed and then just nodded. "I do. And your fans do too. We get a lot of requests for your promotional poster to be sent out to fans who can't make it to one of the tour stops."

"Do you do that?"

"Send out the posters?" she asked. He nodded. "Yes, we do. In fact, when you come to Dallas we are probably going to get you and the other rookies to sign a huge stack of the posters for us to keep on hand to send out."

He shook his head. If anyone had ever told him that people were going to be hanging a poster of him on their wall…well, Gage wouldn't have believed it.

It shouldn't have been him on the posters. He knew that's what his dad would say. It should have been Marty. He stood up and walked away from the couch and from Sierra. Went to the plate-glass windows and stared out, not down at the town below him but up at the night sky.

When he'd been little—six or seven—his grandpa had told him that the deceased were special angels that looked over him. And that had been comforting to Gage after his Memaw had died. He'd liked the thought of her watching over him. But now…was Marty up there looking down on him? He didn't know.

His Memaw had loved him and doted on him. Told him not to listen to his dad who always offered "constructive criticism" on everything he did. She'd just loved him and made him feel like he was enough.

He and his brother hadn't been particularly close when he'd died. Gage was the first to admit a lot of that had to do with him and the resentment he'd no longer been able to hide from his brother. He'd done everything that Marty had and done it better. He'd worked hard at school to get better grades. He'd spent hours after the evening chores were done going over tapes of bull riders and sneaking away to practice on the mechanical bull whenever he could.

And none of that had mattered. His dad still didn't see anything Gage had done and the hero worship he'd always had for Marty had soured and turned to resentment.

"Gage? You okay?" Sierra asked from behind him and he didn't turn to look at her because right now he felt like a brat. He wished he could go back to his eighteen-year-old self and warn that cocky kid that he wasn't going to have his older brother around for long.

But he couldn't. So, he stared up at the sky and wondered what Marty would think of all of this. *What do you think, brother?* Not just the stuff with Montez Denim, the other bit with his dad watching Gage ride and thinking he was Marty.

He hadn't heard her move but Sierra wrapped her arms around him from behind, joining her hands together right under his chest, and he felt her rest her head between his shoulder blades.

She didn't say anything, which was precisely what he needed. She just held him without him having to show her how vulnerable he felt and it meant more to him than he wanted to admit it did.

He patted her hands and closed his eyes, knowing that Sierra meant more to him than he should let her. Because if he knew one thing about himself it was that he was good at being stubborn and holding on to things long after he should have let go. It was the one quality he thought made him so damned good on the back of a bull.

But it also made him pretty horrible at relationships.

Chapter Six

"I'LL BE RIGHT back," she said, leaving him in the bedroom and going into the bathroom to change into the negligee that her mom had included in the wardrobe redo. It was one of the few things her mom had purchased that Sierra had kept. Her mom knew what men liked.

Talking about family hadn't lightened the mood at all and she had the feeling that Gage was on the edge of bolting, not just from her room but from the AEBR Tour as well. The demons he'd been running from earlier were back and she wanted to chase them away.

She looked at herself in the mirror, smoothing her hands down the sides of the cream satin shift. It had black lace on the bodice and ended at the top of her thighs. And though she had balked at it when she'd seen it at first, it was really comfortable and when she wore it she felt like a lady.

She looked at herself in the mirror. It was late and she'd had a lot to drink earlier and then the cheeseburger so she thought brushing her teeth again was a good idea, which she did. Then she ran her hands through her hair trying to fluff it up so that it looked less like her normal hair and sexier.

Except it didn't really look sexy to her; it just looked sort of messy. She patted it back in place and then took a deep breath.

She was nervous.

How ridiculous given that they'd already hooked up, but this was different. Earlier in his truck it had all been lust and attraction burning out of control. This was definitely deliberate. She couldn't say she got carried away by the moment the way she had in the truck or even that he had either. He was waiting in her bed and she was standing in here trying to figure out how to go out there and be normal.

She picked her robe up from where she'd left it on the floor, hung it on the hook on the back of the door and then she got the bug to straighten all of the towels until finally she stopped herself.

Enough.

It was time to go into the bedroom. In fact, there was nowhere she'd rather be than in that bed with him. If only she could be cool until she got there.

Now that she started worrying about that she was afraid she'd trip on her way to the bed…oh, great. Now she had to worry about clumsiness.

"Sierra, darlin'?"

He called her by her name. Not just darlin'. He wasn't subbing her for another woman.

"Yes."

Dang. Her voice squeaked up a little on the end of the

word. Just when she was feeling like she was owning this moment, the real Sierra shone through. Nerves had always betrayed her and this evening was no different.

"Are you coming out of there or should I come in and get you?"

"I'm coming," she said. She ran her hands down her hips and then opened the door. He was lying on his side watching the door. Naked.

She swallowed hard as her heartbeat accelerated and everything feminine in her came to attention. Which sounded silly to her own ears. She had always been her own woman. Very confident of herself on her own, but now she realized there was a part of her that could easily belong solely to Gage.

Gage Powell who was more complicated than she'd expected. Grief and survivor's guilt, she'd figured on him carrying around, but there was something else. Something more she couldn't see or understand.

He quirked one eyebrow at her.

"Darlin'?"

"Hmm."

"You okay?"

She flushed. Here she was staring at him like she'd never seen a naked man before. But he was different. There wasn't a thing about Gage that felt like any other guy she'd been with. She wanted more from him than she'd wanted from them.

And not just sex.

Though the sex was explosive and shook her to her core. She'd never have thought she'd do it in a vehicle. But dang that hadn't even fazed her.

Nothing with him did.

She realized then the change was inside of her. Being with him brought out impulses and desires she normally ignored, but she didn't plan on ignoring them anymore.

She needed to own this night. Make the most of it. She pushed aside the image of the two of them driving together down the coast to the next tour date in San Diego. There was nothing more to this than the night they were sharing right now.

She was trying to prove something to herself and the world… She hesitated for a second. Gage really had no place in her life. She shouldn't be doing this. But then she looked over at him.

He was relaxed lying there naked on his side, watching her with a smile playing around his lips, and she knew she wasn't going to walk away. She might have been arguing with herself out of nerves or to make herself feel better later but she didn't care if this was a one-night stand.

"What do you think of this?" she asked. "It's not my usual style."

She put her hand on her hip and stood there in the doorway realizing that there was still some of the shyness she thought she'd gotten rid of.

THE NIGHTGOWN THAT Sierra wore hugged the curves of her breasts and skimmed over her hips. The heated coupling they'd had in the front seat of his truck hadn't satisfied his soul-deep need to explore her body. There was still so much of her he hadn't explored. He rolled to his back and sank deeper into the pillows, watching her as she walked toward him.

She moved like she had earlier in the promotion tent—all easy long-limbed grace. Each step was slowly measured and confident. She was a woman who knew what she wanted and he was the lucky guy she was coming after. Her shoulders were back and her hips swayed sensuously.

His blood felt hotter in his veins, like that moment when he stood next to the chute waiting to get on the back of a bull. Anticipation and excitement roiled through him. An expression of intent spread over her face and he had the feeling that he was not going to be in control of this. He wasn't one for giving over the reins but he might be able to at least let her believe he was in control.

"Finally. I thought you weren't going to come over here," he said.

"I needed to make sure you wanted me," she countered.

"There was never any doubt," he said.

She sunk down next to him on the bed, and as the hem of her negligee rose, she tugged at it revealing a hint of shyness in her eyes.

He knew he needed to lighten the mood. He didn't want her nerves to get the better of them both. He'd always been a live for the moment sort of guy but tonight he sensed that Sierra needed more from him.

More.

Hell and damn. That had almost always been where he failed. He knew it and anyone who'd ever crossed his path did too. But he wanted to be better for Sierra.

"Want me to show you how to mount a bull?" he asked.

Her eyebrows shot up and she gave him a quizzical look. "Uh, what?"

"Climb on my lap and I'll show you," he said.

"Oh, no, not yet," she said.

He arched one eyebrow at her. "Do you have something else in mind?"

"Uh, well, how about you stay there and I do this?"

He growled deep in his throat when she leaned forward to brush kisses against his chest. Her lips were sweet and not shy as she explored his torso. Then he felt the edge of her teeth as she nibbled at his pecs.

He watched her, his eyes narrowing and his erection hardening. Her tongue darted out and brushed against his nipple. He arched off the bed, and put his hand on the back of her head, urging her to stay where she was.

She straddled him and rested her weight on her hands against his shoulders. Their eyes met and then she slowly let her hand drift down his body, touching him so lightly that he almost felt like it wasn't real. All of his life had been so hard and now there was Sierra with her soft and shy touches.

He tried so hard to just sit back and let her have her way with him. When she reached the edge his belly button, she ran her finger around the rim of it and he felt an answering excitement lower as his cock stirred. Sierra lifted her fingers from his body, looking up at him.

Her touch drifted lower, going to his erection, brushing over his straining length. "I guess you liked that."

"Hell, yeah," he said, pulling her to him. He lifted her slightly so that the tips of her breasts brushed his chest.

"Now it's my turn," he said.

She nibbled on her lips as he rotated his shoulders so that his chest rubbed against her breasts.

"I like that," she said.

Blood roared in his ears. He was so hard, so full right now that he needed to be inside of her body.

Impatient with the fabric of her shift, he shoved it up and out of his way. He caressed her thighs. God, she was soft. She moaned as he neared her center and then sighed when he brushed his fingertips across the crotch of her panties.

The cotton was warm and wet. He slipped one finger under the material and hesitated for a second, looking down into her eyes.

Her eyes were heavy-lidded. She bit down on her lower

lip and he felt the minute movements of her hips as she tried to move his touch where she needed it.

He was beyond teasing her or prolonging anything. He plunging two fingers into her. She squirmed against him.

He pulled her head down to his so he could taste her mouth, which opened over his and he told himself to take it slow, but just like when he drew a bull that was unpredictable, he couldn't stop his gut instincts.

Which demanded he take her as hard and deep as he could. He didn't want to make it last. He was holding on for the ride of his life.

He caressed her back and spine, scraping his nails down the length of it, following it to the indentation above her backside.

She closed her eyes and held her breath as he fondled her, running his finger over her nipple. It was velvety compared to the satin smoothness of her breast. He brushed his finger back and forth until she bit her lower lip and shifted on his lap. He wanted to give her this pleasure because he wasn't too sure of anything beyond this moment. He'd been living from one second to the next and now he felt a pang in his heart at the thought of not spending more time with her. But who knew how much longer he could keep up the charade.

She moaned a sweet sound that he leaned up to capture with his mouth. She wrapped her arms around him and held him close to her as she shifted against him, rubbing against him.

He held her still with a hand on the small of her back. He buried his other hand in her hair and arched her over his arm. Both of her breasts were thrust up at him. He wanted Sierra more than he had wanted any other woman in a long time.

He kept kissing and rubbing, caressing her nipples until her hands clenched in his hair and she rocked her hips harder against his length. He lifted his hips, thrusting up against her. He bit down carefully on her tender, aroused nipple. She screamed his name and he hurriedly covered her mouth with his, wanting to feel every bit of her passion.

Rocking her until the storm passed and she quieted in his arms. He held her close, her bare breasts brushing against his chest. He was so hard he thought he'd die if he didn't get inside her.

He glanced down at her and saw she was watching him. The fire in her eyes made his entire body tight with anticipation.

He didn't want to break the mood so he just reached for the condom he'd brought with him and put it on. He'd thought of the many things going on his life at the moment and he didn't want to bring Sierra into the mess, but he hadn't been able to leave her either.

He needed to be inside her now. He shifted and lifted her thighs, wrapping her legs around his waist. Her hands fluttered between them and their eyes met.

He held her hips steady and entered her slowly. Thrust deeply until he was fully seated. Her eyes widened with each inch he gave her. She clutched at his hips as he started thrusting. Holding him to her, eyes half closed and her head tipped back.

She started to tighten around him. Her hips moving faster, demanding more but he kept the pace slow, steady. Wanting her to come before he did.

He suckled her and rotated his hips with each thrust and he felt her hands in his hair, clenching as she threw her head back and her climax ripped through her.

He wanted to plunge into her again and again until everything exploded around them. But he knew if he could hold on to his control he'd give her more pleasure and that mattered more to him at this moment. He'd been running for so long he craved someone to hold on to. Damn. Could that person be Sierra?

Leaning back on his haunches he tipped her hips up to give him deeper access to her body. He felt the bite of her nails on his back as she drew them slowly down his body, making a mockery of his control. His hips jerked forward with more strength than before. She cupped his ass and held him closer to her. His pulse pounded in his ears and he stopped thinking, could do nothing more than feel Sierra. She was it.

He groaned deep from the center of his soul and then collapsed on her, trying not to crush her. He rolled to his side, holding her closer than he should.

She'd brought him completely out of himself and into a spot where he'd never thought he'd be. He felt like he was enough. That he didn't need to keep searching, but he knew that was just because she was different from other women.

She shifted away from him, curling onto her side as she drifted off to sleep and he wondered if once again he was projecting his emotions onto someone else.

The truth was he still hadn't found a home. He'd found good sex. That was different and he needed to remember that.

Chapter Seven

TOSSING AND TURNING in the unfamiliar bed, his sleep was restless and the images that plagued him were strong.

Gage climbed into the chute and started to adjust his rope. The bull was blowing hard and he could tell it was going to be a rough ride. The bull wasn't one from Harper's breeders but instead had the look of a rougher animal. It reminded him of the one he'd ridden back when he'd been in junior rodeo at about age thirteen. That one had bucked him so hard he'd broken his ribs.

He glanced over to tell his spotter to give him more rope so he could adjust the slack and looked straight into his brother's eyes. Marty had on the same battered hat he'd always worn when they practiced on the ranch.

"Don't screw this up," Marty said, pushing his hat back on his forehead, staring at Gage with that solid, serious gaze of his.

God, he'd missed his brother, but Marty was here. "The ride? I won't. I know what I'm doing."

"Not the ride, little bro. Life," Marty said.

"What?" Gage asked and just then the chute opened and the bull charged out of the pen. Bucking hard enough to jar Gage off his back. He flew through the air landing hard on his back and blinking his eyes as he saw his brother standing over him.

"You don't have this. You need to concentrate."

He blinked again and then opened his eyes. He was in bed with Sierra curled against his side and the dark hotel room ceiling above him.

What the f—?

He was sweating and his heart was racing as if he'd really been thrown by his ride so he carefully got out of the bed and made his way to the adjoining bathroom, picking up his robe on the way.

He closed the door quietly behind him. Sierra had left the night-light on in the bathroom so he could see his own reflection in the large mirror over the sink. He let the robe fall to the floor and put his hands on the marble counter.

Was he losing his mind?

Staring at his own face wasn't going to give him any answers. Hell, he probably was halfway to crazy town. No sane man would pretend to be his deceased brother just to see a look of pride in his father's eyes.

Maybe that was what Marty had meant. It was hard to tell and he wasn't really up for trying to decipher his own dreams. He had never had any that he wanted to remember and he could do without this one lingering.

He turned on the water tap and splashed his face, hoping that would rinse away the last of the dream. He dried his face off and then reached for the robe on the floor, put it on.

What was he doing here with Sierra?

She was his sponsor. And he knew he couldn't treat this like a casual hookup. Though to be honest he'd never had any other type of relationship with women. He just wasn't the put down roots and let's make plans for next month kind of guy.

She hadn't indicated she wanted more than something casual from him. But everything about her made it obvious she wasn't a casual lay. She was serious and steady. She'd said herself that her sister thought she didn't act her age.

And that didn't bother Gage at all.

What bothered him was he liked her.

He wanted to somehow change in this one moment the man he was. Change the way he never could do anything right and maybe figure out a way to stay.

Except he couldn't.

He needed to concentrate and keep on winning.

So Daddy will like you.

He glanced over his shoulder. Damn that had sounded like Marty's voice. But it was only in his head. His brother's ghost wasn't haunting him in Sacramento. It was his own conscience riding him about the mistakes he'd made.

He wasn't even sure if he was riding for himself or for his dad. Which was beyond…well just beyond. But he did know he loved being back here. Being on tour made him feel alive in a way that working on the oil rigs never had. Here he wasn't the odd one out. Everyone on the tour from the three Brazilian rookies to the old dogs had bumps and bruises on the inside and out.

He'd found a home…sort of.

And Sierra?

Hell, tonight he couldn't think. He'd started out wanting to fight to this. He felt that restlessness stirring in him again and knew he should get out of here before he couldn't control it. Until his temper and his own self-destructiveness got the better of him.

He opened the door and glanced over at the bed where she lay sleeping. She looked so small on the bed. Curled toward his pillow, her hair fanned out on her own. He stood there and just watched her. Wanted something that he knew he really couldn't have.

He needed to have his own shit together before he did anything like this again. Especially with her.

It was one thing to hook up with the buckle bunnies who knew the score and had the same expectations, but it was something different to sleep with Sierra.

He turned on his heel, walking out into the main area of the suite where his clothes were neatly piled near the closet by the door and he got changed as quickly and quietly as he could.

He let himself out of the room and took the stairs instead

of the elevator to the lobby. It was quiet at this time of the morning and chilly as he stood at the valet stand waiting for his truck.

As he drove away from the hotel, he didn't look back. He'd walked away from people and places before. And always it had been for the best. Not for himself but for those he'd left behind. He knew his own strengths and weaknesses better than anyone.

SIERRA WOKE UP alone. She rolled over, felt the cold sheets and realized that Gage had been gone for a while. Glancing at the nightstand she saw that it was nearly seven. He probably had some ritual things that like he liked to do before he rode on Saturday. Many of the guys did and she got that.

She got out of bed and saw her nightie on the floor and picked it up, putting it on before she went into the main living area of the suite. She saw his robe in a pile by the front door and went to pick it up. She brought it to her nose and sniffed it before she realized what she was doing and tossed it over the back of the love seat in the living area.

Last night had been great fun. She had to keep thinking of it in those terms. She hadn't been looking for anything from him and she was okay with the fact that he was gone.

Really, she was.

She shook her head as she went to her in-room Keurig machine and powered it up to make a cup of coffee.

She wasn't okay with it.

Lying to herself wasn't going to make the sinking feeling in the pit of her stomach go away. She knew that. She'd never been the kind of woman who thought about temporary. Even in college she'd avoided the mid-term stress-relieving hookups that some of her sorority sisters swore by. She just didn't have time for that.

She liked to think she was more mature than that. But this morning feeling sorry for herself because she was alone, she realized she wasn't.

Her room phone rang and she reached over to get it. Heart racing as she hoped it was Gage.

"Hello."

"Hey, sis. I heard you sent Bruce packing last night. About time someone did. I hate the way he just creeps around watching us while we work. Do you want to grab breakfast before we head back to the tour grounds?"

She swallowed her disappointment. Focusing instead on the positives. Her job. "I know Bruce is only doing his job, but Dad either trusts us or he doesn't. I do have time for breakfast but need to hop in the shower real quick. Want to meet in thirty minutes?"

"Late start for you," Savanna said. "And do you really get ready in thirty?"

"Yeah. The longest bit is blow-drying my hair," she said.

"How about I order room service and have it delivered to your room?" Savanna said. "That way we don't have to wait for a table downstairs."

"Perfect," Sierra said. They had exchanged extra keys yesterday so they could let themselves into each other's rooms. "Come over when you're ready."

"See ya soon," Savanna said.

Sierra hung up the phone and left her half-drank cup of coffee on the side table, going into her room to shower and dress. She put on her makeup, dried her hair and almost convinced herself she was back to normal until she walked into the living area and saw Savanna sitting on the sofa with Gage's robe draped behind her.

She had the TV on the sports channel that was covering the American Extreme Bull Riders Tour and it was playing highlights. She watched the footage from the ring for a moment before her sister turned and saw her standing in the doorway.

"I guess you weren't alone last night, which explains the slow start this morning," she said.

"How do you know it's not my robe?" Sierra asked, putting in one of the earrings she had carried in her hand.

"It smells like aftershave and a little bit like sex," Savanna said. "I'm not judging. It's about time you started enjoying the perks of working with these guys."

"Well, it's not like that."

"It's not?" Savanna asked.

Thankfully there was a knock at the door before her sister could ask anything else. Sierra booked it to let the room service guy in with their breakfast, directing him to set it up in the dining area and then signing the check. The breakfast under the cloches smelled delicious and she realized that she was starving.

"Do you want to talk about him?" Savanna said as she came over and sat down at one of the places.

"No, I don't," Sierra said. "Did we both get the same thing?"

"Yes," Savanna said. "Spinach and egg white omelet with avocado toast."

"Thanks, sis."

"No problem," Savanna said. "It was a guy from the tour, right?"

"Savanna, please."

"Okay, I won't ask anything else," she said. "I'm just surprised and the way you're acting makes me a little bit concerned about you."

"Don't be. It wasn't anything other than some fun. I was ticked off about Bruce and he was running from something as well. We just went out drinking and dancing and had some fun."

Savanna started eating her breakfast.

"Fun is good. Mom is coming down tonight. She wants us to go to dinner together. Are you available?"

She had forgotten about that. Given that Gage had left

she was pretty sure she was available for dinner with her mom and sister. "Of course."

She turned the conversation to the events they had planned for the day and tried to focus on her family and her job. Last night was in the past and she needed to leave it there. Gage had done her a favor by leaving because it would have been a hundred times more awkward if he'd been in the room when Savanna had called.

Or so she thought until she got to the tour grounds and couldn't find Gage anywhere. And when he came out for his ride, their eyes met for a split second and then he looked away. He rode well scoring high in the points table and she thought about going to talk to him; but as she approached the riders' area she noticed a bevy of buckle bunnies hanging around waiting for the riders and made herself walk past.

GAGE WAS BACK in the dressing room before finals in Sacramento. He'd had a good ride earlier and knew he'd gotten lucky that he'd drawn a good bull to ride. Because his concentration hadn't been worth shit. He'd seen Sierra in the stands. Noticed how pale and fragile she looked and then turned away from her. He had a fan event later but he was trying to figure out how to avoid her there. He wasn't ready to talk to her.

At first leaving had seemed the right thing to do. Hell he

still thought it was but now that he was faced with the reality of seeing her again, he knew that he'd screwed up last night.

Big time.

He should have stuck to riding. He should have just walked right past her instead of kissing her and taking her dancing. He should have—but he hadn't. So here he was looking like some damned rookie who'd been bucked off his first ride and hoping like hell no one noticed.

He was looking at the rope in his hands like it held some kind of answer. It didn't. He worked over the frayed edges until he had the rope the exact way he liked it. He remembered the first time he'd done this.

Marty had been standing over him talking him through it.

Don't cut it too close. Trim a little more off there. Okay you got it. Run it through your hands to make sure it feels right.

He'd forgotten the good times with his brother. Had allowed his father's words at the hospital that day to steal his brother from him. All Gage could remember was how he'd been the one alive and his dad had wanted him and Marty to switch places. And that had poisoned his memories of Marty.

But being on the tour was bringing back the good times. When they'd been younger and Marty had been his hero. He'd followed his brother everywhere he went. Marty had been ten years Gage's senior and most of the time Marty didn't mind it.

He'd always been patient and kind. Everything that their

father hadn't been. Gage got it. He understood that his birth had been really hard on his mom and that she'd almost died after he'd been born. It made sense to him that his father would resent him. Plus he'd already had a perfect son.

One whose shadow Gage still felt like he stood in.

He rubbed the back of his neck.

F—.

He remembered his dream…hell, it haunted him. Marty telling him not to screw up.

What would his brother really say if he were here?

He felt that pang in his chest as he realized again how much he missed his brother. He got up and left the dressing room, went into the hallway where he was alone. He needed to talk to someone. Not his brother's ghost or even his dad. He wanted to talk to Nick. His brother's best friend had taken on the role of surrogate brother to Gage without either of them planning on it.

Nicholas Blue had started riding about the same time as Marty and they'd traveled together everywhere. Gage had always trailed along behind them when they were in Oklahoma but when Marty had died…Nick had lost it. He'd left the rodeo and disappeared. Kind of the same way that Gage had. Except that Nick had inherited a chunk of a huge ranch in Whiskey River and a fourth of the Kelly Boots empire. Nick had settled down since Marty had died. He had his daughter Martina and his barrel-racing wife, Reba, and a breeding program that he'd been trying to get off the ground for a little over a year now.

Gage went to his gear, digging out his cell phone and messaged Nick.

> **Gage:** Hey. Getting ready to ride and can't shake the feeling that something's off.

Dancing dots appeared in the response window.

> **Nick:** The finals can do you like that. Take a deep breath. Now picture yourself in the chute on the bull.

Gage tipped his head back and closed his eyes. He took a deep breath in and then let it out. He did what Nick said and imagined the feel of the rope around his gloved hand and the muscled power of the bull between his legs as it got ready to bolt.

He went through the ride in his head. Moving with the bull and staying on until the end. He opened his eyes.

> **Gage:** Thanks. Needed that.
>
> **Nick:** That's what bros are for. Are you coming to WR soon? Martina misses her favorite Unca.
>
> **Gage:** Ha. I hope you mentioned to Xander that I'm the favorite.
>
> **Nick:** I did. So when can we expect you?
>
> **Gage:** I'm in El Paso at the end of August. I could stop by after that.
>
> **Nick:** It's a plan. Good luck on your ride today.
>
> **Gage:** Thanks.

He got up and put his phone back in his bag and then paced around the dressing room. Everyone in the room was busy getting their head into the ride. Gage knew better than to stay in the room when he was so on edge. He stepped back out into the hall and paced up and down until he was needed.

He took his ride and it was better than he'd expected. He'd made the most of his eight seconds, scored up in the high eighties, and as he showered and headed to the Montez Denim tent for his meet and greet, he knew that the time for running from Sierra was over. That ride had shown him that he wasn't playing at being a rider; he was one. This was exactly where he was meant to be. And it was time for him to stop phoning it in.

But when he got to the Montez Denim tent Sierra wasn't there. Regret was nothing new to him but this time he felt like he might have let something special slip through his fingers.

Chapter Eight

THE DOWNTOWN DALLAS headquarters of Montez Denim were in a high-rise building that afforded a view of the grassy knoll where the whole John F. Kennedy thing went down. She stood there facing the city, looking down there at the pretty grassy area and the gorgeous sunny, summer day. It was funny how life could change in an instant.

It had been three weeks since she'd seen Gage on the AEBR Tour. One night of crazy, hot passion and then the next morning...well he'd been gone. He'd left her hotel room in the middle of the night and then avoided her the rest of the weekend until her flight on Sunday.

She was hurt and angry. Not even pretending to deny it. She'd done her best to keep her phone far away when she'd gone out for tacos and margaritas the previous night with some of her Dallas friends. But the truth, she'd thought...she'd thought because of her own feelings for Gage that he'd somehow be different.

He probably thought she was no different than Savanna who was truly just looking for a good time. But she'd never been a good-time girl. And now she understood why. She was never going to be casual about sharing her body with a man. Hell, she knew it was only Gage that she wanted. She wouldn't have done it in the front seat of a truck with any other man.

She had thought about texting him. She had the numbers of the bull riders who were sponsored by the company, but she couldn't make herself do it. It felt like he'd sent her a message and the least she could do was respect it.

So, she was. Besides it wasn't as if they'd started a relationship. She was the first to admit she'd been acting out against her life. Her father's lack of faith in her ability to run the campaign, her sister saying that good girls finish last, her own fear that life was passing her by and she was making sacrifices for nothing.

But today it felt empty.

She tried to tell herself it had nothing to do with the fact that Gage was up at the top of the leader board again. And that she'd spent the last three days in meetings where his picture was on every presentation deck she looked at or flashed on the walls of the hallway outside her office.

Her father and the board had been singing her praises with the campaign, which they'd snickered at to begin with, thinking that the target market for the Extreme denim line was men and they wouldn't respond to half-naked bull riders. But she'd stuck to her guns, knowing women would want their men to wear the brand and men would want to be associated with those young, badass bull riders.

And she'd been right.

There was a knock on her door and she turned away from the window, moving to her chair as she called out for the person to enter.

It was her dad.

He was tall at almost six foot and looked comfortable in what he liked to call western casual. He wore a pair of the Montez Legacy denim jeans, a designer dress shirt, a pair of Kelly Boots. She knew he had a black Stetson in his office. He held a tablet in one hand as he walked toward her.

"Sierra, I need you on a Skype call. I hope you don't mind. I had Bruce check with Marcos and he said you were free for twenty minutes before you had to go and talk to one of the accounts."

"I am. My meeting is a video call as well, so I can probably talk for eighteen of those twenty minutes."

"Just what I was hoping you'd say."

He went to the small love seat and guest chairs set in a conversation area in her office and set the tablet up on the tripod she had situated there for these video calls. Because of the nature of her job she spent a lot of time in meetings and the area she had set up was designed so that she could change out the background depending on the account or partner they were working with.

"Who are we talking to? I can change our backdrop."

"Gage Powell," he said. "Why isn't his picture on your

wall anyway?"

Because every time she looked at him she wanted to punch him or tear his clothes off and neither was suitable for a productive day at the office.

But she couldn't say that to her father.

"I'm set up for my meeting with the account," she said. She would be speaking to one of the major retailers who carried Montez jeans. And while it would probably be advantageous to have Gage's backside behind her during the call, she was honest and admitted that staring at him all day was making her think of things she was trying to forget.

"Well switch it to his poster. Let me do it," her dad said. "I asked Marcos to bring us some drinks. Will you go and check on him?"

"I have a mini fridge in here," she said. Her dad still treated the assistants like they were old-fashioned secretaries sometimes. "What do you want to drink?"

"That peach-flavored tea. Put it in one of our—"

"I know, Dad. This isn't my first rodeo."

He winked at her. "I keep forgetting that you're not like Savanna."

She paused as he said that. "Did you think I was?"

"Made sense to me that both you girls would follow after your momma. Though you are a little more...shy I guess is the right word than those two are. But you're just as pretty and men do notice you when you walk in the room."

All that time trying so hard to be different from them

and her father had always just looked at her and saw…girl. No doubt it was the way he looked at all women. She loved him but there were times when she was pretty sure he was stuck in the last century.

She went to the credenza where the mini fridge and Montez logo glasses were. She poured her father's favorite peach tea into one glass and then poured herself some sparkling water and walked over to sit down next to her dad.

"So what's the conversation about?"

"I need you to help me talk Powell into doing a TV ad and probably a web advertising video campaign. He's got a break coming up and I thought you could take a crew to Oklahoma and go film him on his ranch."

Uh, no. She was avoiding him. She'd woken up alone in that big king bed after a night like she'd never experienced before.

But she was a grown-ass woman and she was going to woman up.

Because that idea was gold. Gage was hot right now— not only on the AEBR Tour but with all of their accounts as well.

GAGE HEARD HIS phone make the video call noise and cursed under his breath. The break in the tour after El Paso meant most of the riders went home, but he was avoiding Bar P. So instead he was in Whiskey River, taking a few days to relax with Nick Blue. Nick and his wife Reba had a little two-year-old girl they had named after Marty.

They'd asked him to be the godfather and he'd said yes. He knew that Martina had no real connection to Marty but she always made him remember his brother and not with the anger, guilt and rage that he normally associated with him when he was on tour.

Montez Denim. Damn but Davis Montez was one determined man. He'd already told him no five ways from Sunday but the man just kept on calling.

He hit the answer button and fumbled around to turn on the video. His goddaughter was sitting across the child-sized table from him pouring him a cup of 'tea'.

"I've got to take this call," he said to Reba who was also seated at the table. "Can you save my cookies until I get back?"

"I will try."

"Miss Mousy loves cookies," Martina said, gesturing to her stuffed cat, and Gage suspected it was Martina who loved them.

He stood up as the video came on and walked to the wraparound porch where he could find some privacy. But then he glanced down at the screen and stopped walking.

All he could see was Sierra.

Damn.

He missed her. It was hard for him to admit it, especially

to himself since he'd made a life by staying alone and always leaving. But he'd been unable to keep her from his mind after their night together.

He'd woken up in a cold sweat and realized that his night of fun had turned into something else as he'd watched her sleeping. Something had shifted, revealing the emptiness he hadn't realized he'd been running from. And he realized that he didn't want to let her go.

But he was a man in the middle of something he couldn't stop. A man who wasn't sure who he was anymore. And holding Sierra had made him realize that he might never know again. That everything he'd thought was real had been a chimera. Something false and shining pretending to be the truth when it was nothing but a lie.

"Hello, Gage. I hope we didn't catch you at a bad time," Davis said. "Sierra and I have been talking about how well you are doing on the tour—congratulations by the way—and how well consumers are responding to your ads. We'd like to take it to the next level with some video spots to go along with the print campaign."

"What did you have in mind?" he asked.

"We'd like to film you on the ranch," he said.

"Kind of in your element and emphasizing that you wear the jeans to put in a long day's ranching too. We'd probably want to show you in three environments and then cut it together. So on the tour, at home on the ranch and then out for the night. Montez Denim is the right choice for every part of your life, something like that," Sierra said.

He noticed she'd cut her hair. It now hung to just above her shoulders. He also noticed she was wearing a pair of heavy-rimmed glasses and kept looking at the tablet on her lap instead of up at the screen.

Was she avoiding him?

Hell of course she was. He'd walked out on her. It had to be awkward. He knew how to make a hash out of things, didn't he? This was precisely why he'd left originally.

"I'm not a rancher," he said.

"Well, son, the Powell name is synonymous with bull riding and ranching. Your old man was a champ and your brother—God rest his soul—was on his way to becoming one. We've all seen the Bar P in photos. Could you just let us set up some shots of you out there?"

No. In fact, hell no. But he didn't say that and instead just shook his head.

"We don't want you to be dishonest about who you are, Gage," Sierra said. "But it would make the campaign more cohesive if we could get you out there. We could say downtime and show you practicing for the tour or just riding on the ranch."

She'd leaned in to talk and had removed her glasses. Her hair swung forward and he remembered how it had felt brushing against his skin.

"Okay."

Okay? Where the hell had that come from?

"Great. I will get in touch with our video ad department and assign someone to oversee the production—"

"I don't want anyone but you, Sierra. If I'm going to do it, I want you to be in charge and to be the one who supervises the filming," he said. He knew he'd screwed up when he left but seeing her again had just reinforced that there was something about her he didn't want to let go of.

"I have other—"

"She'll do it," Davis said. "We will be in touch with the itinerary, but it will probably be quick because we want to get the TV spots booked when the tour starts back up."

"Fine. I'm in Texas right now so I'll need a day or two to get back to the Bar P," he said.

"Can you get to Dallas?"

"Sure, why?"

"You and Sierra can fly up on the corporate jet," Davis said. "I'll be in touch with your management and get the new contract out to you by the end of day. Have a good one."

Davis ended the call but not before he'd seen the look on Sierra's face. She wasn't pleased about flying up in the jet with him. He tried to tell himself that it was a good thing she hadn't looked angry. But a part of him wondered if the emotions she'd stirred in him were one-sided. And if they were…well, he'd faced down worse situations and brought them around his way.

Now that he'd seen her again he was determined to convince her to give him another shot.

"GOOD JOB, GIRL. I thought we were losing him but you talked him around to our thinking. I've already sent you an email with my thoughts, but this campaign has been your baby so I'm sure you'll come up with something brilliant," her dad said moving ahead with the same lightning speed he always used.

"I'm sure I will," she said. "Dad, I really can't go to Oklahoma or on the tour with Gage. I have other accounts that I have to take care of."

"This is the priority, Sierra. Maybe you can let Marcos take a stab at covering some of them while you are working on this. I don't think it will be more than a few days. We have to move quickly and if Gage wants you on the shoot than that's what we are going to give him. I'm going to talk to legal to get the contract drawn up. Why don't you talk to creative and get some storyboards ready?"

"Thanks, Dad, like I don't know how to work on TV spots."

"Never hurts to have a reminder," he said with a wink before he walked out the door, closing it behind him.

Most of her life had been like this with that man. He came into her day like a tornado, stirring everything up, and then left just as quickly never seeing the destruction he left behind.

Though she knew this was a mess of her own making. She'd been the one to talk Gage into going out with her that night. She'd gone with him. She'd danced with him like she was young and free when she'd never been anything other than a forty-year-old trapped in a twenty-year-old's body according to Savanna. And right now she'd have to agree with her older sister.

She had regrets. Most of them centered around not tracking Gage down—just letting him walk away. She'd let him treat her like she was disposable and he had. She should have had a conversation with him over the weekend in Sacramento instead of just waiting for him to come to her. Maybe she'd watched too many period dramas on PBS but just once she wanted a relationship to work the way they did in books and movies. She wanted the guy to somehow twig she wanted more than just one night of fun.

Oh, God, what if he wanted to hook up again?

What if now he thought she was his booty call?

She groaned and fell against the back of the love seat, staring at the ceiling. She was making herself crazy. And hot. Just thinking of being back in Gage's bed was enough to awaken all the desires she'd been steadily denying she had. All the longings that had kept her up at night and avoiding looking at his picture in the hallway of the office building.

And now she was going to have to spend at least five days alone with him…and a film crew. She was going to have to be professional.

Anything else would be…

Well that didn't bear thinking about.

Her door opened and Marcos walked in. "You've got five minutes until the conference call. I have Abi and Taylor on their way up from creative."

"Thanks, Marcos. Do you think you can start the call for me? You've been working with me on this project so maybe you can take the lead on it."

"I'd love to," Marcos said. "I guess there is more going on with the AEBR campaign."

"More than I have time to explain in five minutes."

"Margaritas after work?" he said.

Marcos was more than her assistant; he was one of her best friends. He was smart and funny and had the knack for saying just the right thing at the right time.

"We're going to be here late."

"All the more reason to go out after," he said.

She gathered her notes for the call and went over them briefly with Marcos just as Abi and Taylor arrived. Her afternoon was busy, filled with meetings and calls with little time to do anything other than focus on the many tasks she had on her to-do list. But memories of Gage teased her constantly. Making it hard for her to pay attention. She knew she needed to figure out how to face him and stop the fixation she had on him.

There was only one person who could give her any kind

of advice and that was Savanna. She'd gone to New Orleans with the Brazilian riders who wanted to party and Sierra wasn't too sure that calling her sister and asking for advice was the wisest thing. And despite what Marcos had said, by the time they finished mapping out the work for the next two weeks and making plans for her to shoot the TV spots it was late and Marcos's husband had come home early from a business trip.

He'd offered to hang out with her, but she knew he wanted to get home and had let him off the hook.

Instead she sat in her apartment with an unopened bottle of tequila, remembering the way Gage's hands had felt on her skin and the way his lips had tasted. She spent a restless night telling herself that one time was enough and that seeing him again was going to be just fine. But lying to herself in the middle of the night wasn't something she'd ever been able to do. She knew that she was riding straight toward a big ol' heartache unless she could figure out a way to make Gage unappealing.

Chapter Nine

G AGE LEFT WHISKEY River two days later. Driving up to Dallas gave him time to think and clear his head. He was riding better than he'd expected. He was pleased with his place near the top. This break was for twelve days and the last thing he wanted to do was fly to his parents' ranch with Sierra so he'd countered with picking her up in his truck.

After two days in Whiskey River visiting with Nick, Reba and his goddaughter two-year-old Martina he was the most mellow he could be. They were the people who made him feel like it was okay to just be himself.

It was only a six-hour drive to his folks' place from the Dallas area and she'd agreed.

They still hadn't talked. Not really. He'd been part of a number of email chains about the new shooting schedule and what he should wear and he even got to weigh in on the model that he'd been out on the town with in one part of the photo shoot. That part they were going to do in Fort Worth at Billy Bob's Texas, which was owned by Willie Nelson and had a mechanical bull, live music and other amusements. They were going to be shooting in the middle of the afternoon so would have the place to themselves.

It was odd.

They were making up a life for him and because he knew it was just for an advertising campaign it didn't bother him the way it did when he dwelled on the fact that his dad thought he was Marty.

He'd talked to Nick about it who despite being pretty fun-loving and always goofing on everyone had a solid head on his shoulders. Nick had said that family was complicated. God knew Nicholas Blue knew that better than many. He'd found out he was the illegitimate son of Boots Kelly after the old man had died and left him a legacy that included a share in the world-famous boot-making company and a stake in the Kelly ranch in Whiskey River.

Nick, who'd been drifting a little after Marty's death, had gone to Whiskey River and Reba had found him there. Nine months later they'd had a daughter and they'd had to figure out how to work as a family.

He'd just told Gage that the only person whose opinion mattered was his own. Only he could say what was right for himself when it came to his own father. And that had resonated with him.

Gage stopped feeling like a fool and stared feeling like he was doing the only thing he could. He had always craved his father's love and attention and he had it now. And somehow seeing him ride was making his dad happy. Was helping him through the worsening of his condition. Every day he forgot more things according to Gage's mom but when he watched Gage ride he seemed himself. Those were her words.

He rubbed the back of his neck as he pulled into the parking garage underneath the Montez Denim building. He was going to have to tell Sierra about his dad before they got to the ranch. He knew that. And he still wasn't sure how he was going to do it.

Nick knew his dad, had known Marty, so he got the whole family dynamic without needing a bunch of explaining. What would Sierra think when he told her?

He didn't know. Hell, she might not even feel like talking to him. He was getting a definite chilly vibe off of her.

He got out of the truck and took the elevator up to her floor. He walked into the reception area where three people were seated. Two women and a man. They all looked up when he got off the elevator. He felt uncomfortable as he noticed a huge poster of him in Montez jeans—no shirt, looking over his shoulder—was mounted behind the reception desk.

He cursed under his breath.

"I guess we can rule out airbrushing on the poster," one of the women said with a wink. "Nice to meet you in the flesh, Gage."

He walked over to her. She had short blonde hair with one strand dyed an Easter egg pink color and she had bright violet eyes. Her eyes were rimmed in a thin line of kohl eyeliner and she had an easy, flirty smile.

"Hello…" He glanced down at the desk but there was no nameplate.

"Milly," she said. "Are you here to see Sierra?"

"I am," he confirmed.

She typed something on her keyboard and then waited and typed again.

"Someone from that department will be down in a few minutes to get you. Can I get a selfie?"

He nodded and she came around the side of the desk and posed with him. He avoided looking at himself in the viewfinder and smiled as she snapped two or three photos.

"Thanks."

"No problem," he said as the elevator pinged and the doors opened. Sierra walked out of the car. She was dressed in a form-fitting dress that technically could be called office appropriate and he guessed it would be if he didn't know the body beneath it intimately. But it hugged her curves and accentuated the fullness of her breasts and all he could think of was that she wasn't giving off the icy vibe now.

"Sierra."

"Gage. Thanks for coming by the office," she said. "Do you want to follow me and we'll head up to the meeting? Some of the team had an idea this morning for some new still photos. I hope you won't mind indulging them. I know the new contract mentioned the possibility of a photo shoot."

"I'm not going to hold you to the letter of the contract,"

he said.

"Thank you for that," she said, stepping into the elevator and hitting a button.

He didn't see which one because he was busy staring at her. Reminding himself of details he'd forgotten like the tiny birthmark on the side of her neck and the way she tucked her hair behind her ear when she was nervous.

The doors closed and she crossed her arms over her chest and looked over at him. There was something in her eyes that should have been a warning.

"So, was I just a booty call?" she asked.

HE REACHED AROUND her and pushed the stop button, glancing over his shoulder at her. She had her arms crossed over her chest, which emphasized the curves of her breasts. Her hair was pulled back in some sort of updo that he didn't know the name for and she had on makeup but it was understated and highlighted her prettiness.

She was staring at him expecting an answer and he couldn't help but think she was also angling a little bit for a fight.

"I thought that was what you wanted."

She wrinkled her brow and shook her head. "I...how did you get that?"

"The entire evening felt like one big change. Like we

were both searching for something that we couldn't really find and then after…hell, I'm not good at this. I'm going to say something that convinces you I'm a jerk."

She tipped her head to the side studying him for a long moment and he wondered why he'd ever come back from Scotland. On the rig he'd be doing his thing with a bunch of guys who didn't want to do anything except work, drink and get laid when they were on shore leave.

"I don't think you're a jerk. I'm just trying to make sense of this."

"I can't help there. I left like I did because the entire night wasn't real. I'm on the tour to win, not sleep with sponsors, and I know you weren't looking to hook up either." He took his hat off, ran his fingers through his hair and then looked over at her. "Plus, I didn't know what to say. I figured if you wanted more than what we'd had you would come and find me. It's not like you don't know where I am."

She let her arms fall to her sides. "Are you saying you felt like I just wanted to get laid?"

"No. See this is why I didn't want to talk. I suck at discussing things," he said, stepping closer to her. "I like you, Sierra, but we work together and I'm dealing with some other things that make me more like a dangerous bull than a good ride. I'm just trying to keep either of us from being gored."

She reached up and touched the side of his face. Her fingers were cold and light as she cupped his jaw and then she went up on tiptoe and kissed him softly and gently before stepping back. "Thank you for that."

She reached around him and hit the button to make the elevator start moving again and didn't say another word. When the doors opened she walked past him and after putting his Stetson back on he followed her. He had no idea if anything was resolved or really where they stood.

She led him to a large room similar to the one where he did the original photo shoot and he was whisked away by the hair and makeup person. Damn if he wouldn't get the crap ribbed out of him if his friends knew he was having makeup put on. But he just went where he was bid, trying to make sense of what had happened in the elevator.

He had plenty of time to think since the photographer wanted him to pose and stare broodingly off in the distance. The more they moved him around and posed him the more he thought that he was damned glad this wasn't how he made a living because he'd never be able to do this full-time.

He scanned the crowd for a glimpse of Sierra but she wasn't anywhere to be found. Nothing had been resolved by their little elevator chat. Maybe that conversation had given her the closure she needed. He'd left her in the early morning hours to avoid the chat he'd just been forced to endure.

Talking never did do him a bit of good and this was no exception. After four hours, they finally were done and he was told he could change and that someone would meet him in the boardroom to go over the photo shoot the next day. He had been so fixated on seeing her again it hadn't occurred to him what he'd do when he did see her. She wasn't going to just be all let's hit the sheets again. She had too much class for that. Hell, she probably had too much class for him.

"Do you want to see the contact sheet from your shoot?" Sierra asked from the doorway.

"Sure. Did they turn out okay?" he asked, realizing that he—who'd never been nervous about anything, not facing down a tough bull or even flying through a North Atlantic storm to an oil rig—was nervous around her.

He'd tried to tell her how he felt, botched it as usual, but inside of him he still wanted her. And not just for sex. Though one night had definitely not been enough to sate his need for her. He wanted to sit and talk to her, to try to figure out what was going on between them and if when this AEBR Tour was over there was a shot for them.

But then he stopped his thoughts. A shot for them to do what? He was leaving the US after this tour. He wasn't hanging around to watch the father he couldn't ever figure out how to love to sink deeper into a disease where he recognized him less and less. And his mom…well she had her family near her and she had the ranch. It was home to her. But it hadn't been home to him in a long time.

"Gage?"

"Huh?"

"You coming?"

"Yeah," he said, putting his hat on and following her out of the room. He wished he could look at Sierra the way he did a bull before he got on the back of it. Analyze her strengths and weaknesses and figure her out. But he couldn't. She confused him and made him want to be something he was damned sure he wasn't.

SHE'D GOTTEN THE answer she thought she'd wanted from Gage so leaving him at his hotel and going home should have been easy enough. But instead she found herself coming up with ways to prolong the night and he didn't seem to mind.

She knew he wasn't ready for anything more than that one night they'd had together. She'd seen his face in the elevator and could easily read between the lines. Whatever was going on in his life it was complicated and she didn't want to add to the pressure. Aside from the fact that if she distracted him and he dropped in the ranking before the new TV ads ran her dad would kill her.

Dinner at the Dallas area eatery was a lively affair with a few of the team from creative team at Montez Denim going along. Despite how Gage was one-to-one sort of quiet, in a group he was pretty funny and talkative. She had deliberately made sure she sat at the opposite end of the table from him, which had been a mistake because she'd had no choice but to watch him all night.

And as the evening had worn on, her resistance to him had worn down. So, when they were outside waiting for the valet to bring their cars and discussing who should take Gage back to his hotel room, she'd blurted out that she would.

Which had earned her an odd look from Marcos who lived closer to the hotel than she did.

"I want a chance to go over some logistics for when we get up to your ranch," Sierra said.

And Marcos had winked at her before getting into his car and driving off.

"Do you mind?" she asked Gage.

"Not at all. I'm happy to answer all of your questions," he said.

He got into the passenger side of her sports car. She got in on the driver's side and then as she sat behind the wheel she realized that she didn't have the wild out of control feeling that had ruled her the last time she was with Gage. Instead she felt solid and sure.

There was something about him that made her want to get to him know better. She didn't want him to be her guilty pleasure anymore. And there had been way too much guilt over the last few weeks while they'd been apart.

"What kind of music do you like?"

"Anything," he said.

She hit the button on her steering wheel and the local top 40 station came on. She pulled away from the restaurant, carefully maneuvering her way through traffic to the highway so she could head toward downtown and his hotel.

"I lied about needing to talk to you about the ranch," she said. "I just wanted to be alone with you."

"I know."

"Really? I didn't even know until I said it."

He nodded. "We spent all night looking at each other and pretending we weren't. There is something between us, darlin'."

There was. Right now, it was bordering on some kind of obsession for her. She wanted to pretend it was because of the last few weeks. Her staring at his picture all the time and him being absent from her life. But she knew it was more than that.

"This is crazy. I can tell you don't want to get involved. And honestly, I've just managed to earn the respect of the board so starting something with you isn't exactly going to help me maintain it."

He turned in the seat, took his Stetson off and set it on his lap. He ran his hand through his hair. "I'm in the same spot."

"How? Everyone thinks you're golden. I'm hoping I don't do anything to mess that up."

He shook his head. "Not everyone. My mom goes back and forth between being scared I'm putting my life on the line and proud that I'm doing so well. When I talked to her after the last win, she admitted she'd watched my ride through her fingers. That she wanted to look away but then was afraid if she didn't watch something would happen to me like it did with Marty."

Her heart broke a little when he said that. She didn't watch him ride anymore either. Now that she'd slept with him and started caring for him it was hard to do.

She reached over and squeezed his shoulder. "I'm sorry. How's your dad taking it?"

"What do you mean?"

"Does he comfort your mom and tell her not to worry?" she asked.

He put his hat back on and turned away from her, looking out the window at the passing landscape as they exited the highway and went past the American Airlines Center. He kept his silence and she realized he wasn't going to say anything else to her.

She wondered what was going on there.

"Sorry if I asked something I shouldn't."

He sighed. "It's not that. My dad and I have never had an easy relationship. And after Marty died…well things didn't get better."

She wondered at that. She would have thought that the senior Powell would have turned his attention to Gage. And she knew from watching the footage that Gage was a gifted rider and seemed to have a natural fluidity that his brother hadn't. Marty had been more physical on the bull, almost as if it had been stubbornness keeping him in place.

"That stinks. Believe me I know how complicated dads

can be."

"You do, don't you?" he asked. "Has your dad ever mentioned that he wished you were more like Savanna?"

She thought about how he'd said that he thought she was like Savanna. "Not in so many words. But he does tend to see us as two peas in a pod. Is that what you meant?"

He shook his head as she pulled into the circle drive in front of his high-rise hotel.

"No. Not that. More like: I wish you were more like your brother," Gage said.

There was a bit of rage and old disappointment in his tone and it broke her heart to hear it.

"That's horrible."

"You don't know the worst of it," he said.

"Want to tell me about it?" she asked. Even though she knew that there was no way she could go into the hotel with him, talk and not spend the night.

Chapter Ten

GAGE HAD NEVER really thought of himself has having a gift for seduction but given the fact that he had Sierra in his hotel room and there were only two things they could do, make love or talk, he was leaning toward making love.

And the last time, the way he'd left made him want to make things up to her. And to himself.

He couldn't walk away from Sierra. He was surprised at how much he needed her. He had always had big appetites and been obsessive once he found something he liked. And he certainly liked her.

"So...about dads," she started and he pulled her into his arms and kissed her.

He knew that if he made this physical then his emotions would recede. And this could be a passionate memory for him to look back on years from now.

Her rich brown hair was caught up in a clip so he reached up and took the clip out of it and fanned it out around her shoulders.

"So, you don't want to talk?" she asked.

"I can't," he said. He stepped back. "Do you want to

go?"

"Are you crazy?" she asked. "But if we do this…I'm not going to wake up alone again am I?"

"No," he promised.

She looked so sophisticated and pretty. In his entire adult life he'd never fit in with her. He was a bull rider and a roughneck. And as he caught a glimpse of the two of them in the mirror over the dresser he felt stronger that she was too good for him.

She'd just asked him if he was going to stay after they had sex… Did he really think he would?

"Why are you here with me?"

She turned in his arms and looked up at him. "I like you. A lot. I think I first started to fall for you when I watched you on TV getting ready for your debut. I…I knew who you were. This cute, up-and-comer that Montez Denim wanted to sponsor and then everything blew up and you disappeared and I forgot about you, Gage, until this year when you were back.

"I guess you were always on my radar. What happened in Sacramento just made me realize there is so much about you I don't know. And I want to know more about you. But only if you are interested in staying."

"I am."

"Promise?"

The hint of vulnerability in her voice got him right in the gut and he knew he couldn't walk away again.

"Promise."

He drew the zipper down at the side of her body and watched as the red material gaped open. He slipped his hand under the fabric and touched her skin.

Her breath caught and she shifted in his arms, moving back to put some space between the two of them. He reached between them and drew her hands up to the first button on his shirt.

Staring into her wide green eyes he saw the shyness that was so much a part of her melt away as her fingers brushed against his chest.

Blood rushed through his veins, hardening in his groin and starting a fire in him as she started unbuttoning his shirt. Her fingers were long and cool against his skin as she worked her way down his body. When she finished unbuttoning the shirt she pushed it open and he shrugged out of it.

He flinched as she touched one of the bruises on his ribs from a fall he'd taken in El Paso during qualifying.

He watched her and his jeans felt too tight. She brushed her tongue against his nipple. He canted his hips forward and put his hand behind her head, urging her to keep going.

"How did you get this bruise?" she asked, her tongue tracing over the skin under his left nipple.

"Took a tumble during qualifying. Guess you were too pissed at me to watch," he said.

"No. Not pissed. Just didn't trust myself to stay away from the tour if I watched you ride, so I've been avoiding it."

"How'd that work for you?"

"I'm here now. So how do you think?" she asked. She had one hand braced on his chest as she leaned over him.

He lifted her up and carried her to the bed and sat down so that she straddled him. He leaned up and kissed her lips.

"I'm sorry. I went to look for you after my finals ride in Sacramento but you were gone."

"It's okay," she said, leaning down to lave the spot with her tongue. "We don't have to keep going over it."

He kissed her again, letting his mouth move down the column of her neck. He'd hurt her without meaning to. Something that he couldn't do again.

She shrugged her shoulders, pulling her right arm out of the dress. The bodice loosened and the other sleeve slid down her left arm until the dress was pooled at her waist. She wore those strapless bra cups that were clear in color. He could see her breasts clearly and yet as he reached up to touch them, he felt only fabric and not the sweetness of her flesh.

He stroked his finger around her breasts. She shivered in his arms and rocked against him. His erection got even harder and he rubbed it against her core. He lifted his hip to tip her body up toward him. He traced the edge of her bra with his tongue.

He rubbed his hands over the length of her naked back. Enjoying the feel of this warm woman in his arms.

She put her hands on his shoulders and eased her way

down his chest. She traced each of the muscles that ribbed his abdomen and then slowly made her way lower. He could feel his heartbeat in his erection and he knew he was going to lose it if he didn't take control.

But another part of him wanted to just sit back and let her have her way with him. When she reached the edge of his pants, she stopped and glanced up his body to his face.

Her hand went to his erection, stroking over his straining length. He reached up and removed the bra she still wore and then lifted her slightly so that her nipples brushed against him.

He shoved the fabric of her dress up to her waist and out of the way. He caressed her thighs. Her skin was soft and his calloused hands felt rough in comparison. He brushed his fingertips across the crotch of her panties, feeling the warm, wet lace. He slipped one finger under the material and paused for a moment.

He pushed the fabric of her panties aside and lightly traced the opening of her body. She was warm and wet and so ready for him. It was only the fact that he wanted her to come at least once before he entered her body that enabled him to keep his own needs in check.

She shifted against him and he entered her body with just the tip of one finger. He teased them both with a few short thrusts.

"Gage…" she said, her voice breathless and airy.

"Yes, darlin'?"

"Enough of this foreplay."

"What did you have in mind?" he asked, pushing his finger deep inside of her.

"That will do," she said, her hips rocking against his finger for a few strokes before she was once again caught on the edge and needing more.

"Gage, please."

He pulled his finger from her body and traced it around her clit. Her eyes widened and she rocked her hips frantically against him. She leaned backward as he caught the tip of one breast between his lips. She braced herself with her hands on his thighs.

He turned his head and drew her beaded nipple into his mouth. Suckled her deeply as he plunged two fingers into her body. He kept his thumb on her clit as he worked his fingers deep inside her until she threw her head back and called his name.

He felt the tightening of her body against his fingers. She kept rocking against him for a few more minutes and then collapsed against him.

He kept his fingers inside of her body and slowly started building her toward the pinnacle again. He tipped her head toward his so he could taste her mouth. Her lips caressed his and he reminded himself to take it slow because Sierra wasn't used to him. But one taste of her lips and he was out of control.

He nibbled on her lips and held her at his mercy. Her

nails dug into his shoulders and she leaned up, brushing against his chest. Her nipples were hard points and he pulled away from her mouth, glancing down to see them pushing against his chest.

She held his shoulders and moved onto him, rubbing her center over his erection.

He reached between them and unzipped his pants, freeing his erection. She moaned as he brushed the tip of his cock against her humid center.

She reached between them and touched him. Her small hand navigated the length of his cock and then she shifted to put the tip of his cock inside her body.

She stayed like that, straddling him so that just the tip of his erection was inside of her.

He scraped a fingernail over her nipple and she shivered in his arms. He pushed her back a little bit so he could see her. Her breasts were full, tempting curves rising up and he held her at her waist, just looking at her and wondering if he was going to be able to control the lust that was threatening his control.

She rocked her hips, trying to take him deeper and he knew the time for teasing was at an end.

"Gage?"

"Hmm?"

"No more teasing," she said.

"No more," he agreed giving her another inch of his cock, thrusting his hips up into her sweet, tight body. Her eyes were closed, her hips moving subtly against him, and when he blew on one nipple he saw gooseflesh spread down her body.

He loved the way she reacted to his mouth on her. He sucked on the skin of her collarbone as he thrust all the way into her. Sheathing the entire length of his cock in her body. He knew he was leaving a mark with his mouth and he was glad. He wanted her to remember that he'd claimed her. The first few times had been fun and spontaneous. This was deliberate. He was claiming Sierra for his own.

"Come with me," he whispered against her skin. He kept the pace slow, building the pleasure between them.

As always when he was with Sierra he was struggling to make it last. But he felt like he was going to lose it. Each time he thought it would be different. That somehow he'd imagined how perfect she fit him. But he was wrong. Each time was more intense.

"Wrap your legs around me."

She did as he asked and he rolled them over so that she was beneath him. He pushed her legs up against her body so that he could thrust deeper. So that she was open and vulnerable.

"Come now, Sierra," he said.

She nodded and he felt her body tighten as she clutched at his hips. Then she scraped her nails down his back, clutched his buttocks and drew him in. His sac tightened and his blood roared in his ears as he felt everything in his world center to this one woman.

He called her name as he came. She tightened around him and he looked down into her eyes as he kept thrusting. He saw her eyes widen and felt the minute contractions of her body around his as she was consumed by her orgasm.

He rotated his hips against her until her hips stopped rocking against him. She wrapped her arms around his shoulders and kissed his chest and then the spot right over his heart.

"Oh, Gage," she said. "Thank you for making love to me."

"You're very welcome, Sierra."

She wrapped her arms around him and held him close. "I'm tired but I don't want to fall asleep. I know this is your hotel room, but that didn't—"

He kissed her to stop the flow of words. He hated hearing her fears, knowing that he was responsible for them. He pulled her closer to him, tucking her head under his chin and running his hand over the back of her head.

"Go ahead. I won't leave you. Remember I promised," he said.

"You did. Are you a man of your word?" she asked.

He hated that she had to ask but didn't blame her. "Yes, I am."

Chapter Eleven

THE RANCH LOOKED big and prosperous as they pulled under the arch with the name Powell emblazoned on it. Sierra looked over at Gage but the fun-loving guy from the night before was gone and in his place was someone…she didn't recognize.

At his request, she'd told the team to give them two days before they joined them for filming. She thought it was the least they could do given that Gage hadn't been home since spring. He had made the comment offhandedly but she could tell that he'd been almost dreading coming home.

As soon as he pulled his truck to a stop in front of the large ranch house, the door opened and an older woman with Gage's blondish-brown hair ran down the porch steps toward the truck.

A huge smile lit Gage's face as he turned off the engine and got out of the cab. He caught his mom as she ran toward him and gave her a big bear hug. Sierra could only sit there and watch with envy. Neither of her parents had ever greeted her that way. But then again she and Savanna were always with one of them. And she knew there was something broken in Gage's family. A wound left by Marty's death that had never healed, she suspected.

She opened her own door and carefully stepped down from the truck.

"Ma, this is Sierra Montez. She's in charge of the PR for my sponsorship deal with Montez Denim. It was her idea to film me here on the ranch. Sierra, this is my mom, Lucinda Powell."

"It's a pleasure to meet you, Mrs. Powell," Sierra said, walking over to them and offering her hand.

Mrs. Powell gave her a warm smile. "Call me Lucy—everyone does."

"Lucy then," she said. "I see Gage favors you."

"That he does. He has his daddy's eyes though."

"How is he today?" Gage asked.

"It's a good day. He's out working with the boys but should be back in soon for supper. You two grab your bags so I can get you settled," Lucy said.

She turned toward the cab but Gage nudged her aside gently. "Ma, I'm a gentleman. I'll get Sierra's bag."

"I wasn't sure," Lucy said.

"That Gage would do it?" Sierra asked.

"That you'd let him. Some city gals like to do it themselves. Ain't nothing wrong with that," she said, holding up her hands.

"No, ma'am, there isn't. But I figure if I got a big strong man like Gage willing to tote my bags for me, I'll let him."

"Makes him feel useful," Lucy said with a wink.

"It does," Sierra said with a smile knowing full well that Gage could hear them.

"Keep it up, ladies, and next time I'll let you both do it yourselves," Gage said.

"Not if you want any cobbler."

"Peach?"

"Does my baby like any other kind?" Lucy asked.

"Well, then, ma'am, I'll be carrying whatever you need me to," Gage said as they entered the house.

The foyer was rustic but modern with hardwood floors that were polished. There was a console table set to one side with a framed picture of the ranch house over it and then on the table was a small framed portrait of Gage and his brother. Neither Lucy nor Gage paused as they entered the house and Sierra dropped back, following them both up the stairs to the second floor.

She listened to them talking quietly about his dad as she walked along the wide hallway. They passed three doors before Gage stopped. "You're in here. This is the guest room."

Lucy opened the door for her and she followed Gage into the room. He put her suitcase next to the dresser. "That door leads to a shared bathroom with my room."

"If you need anything that I haven't provided, let me know," Lucy said. "After you get settled come on down to the back porch and we can sit a spell."

"Yes, ma'am," Sierra said. A moment later she was alone in the guest room. She looked at the antique four-poster bed and the quilt that to her untrained eye looked handmade. She sat down on the queen-sized mattress and it was firm but comfortable as she flopped back and threw her arms out to the sides.

What was she doing here?

Gage had insisted that she come but she knew she could have gotten out of it if she'd wanted to. Instead she'd...well she wanted to be here. Wanted to try to understand why she hadn't heard from him since Sacramento. But more than that she needed to figure out why she wanted to be here. And she did want to be here.

His mom was sweet and her smile when she looked at Gage showed her love and concern for her son. Sierra knew that she could probably figure out a little more of what was going on with Gage from his mom. But she wanted Gage to tell her when he was ready...didn't she?

There was a knock on the door and she realized she'd been staring at the ceiling instead of unpacking.

"Yes?"

"I'm heading down. You ready?" Gage asked.

"Come in," she said.

He opened the door and she noticed he'd taken off his Stetson and his hair was matted around the top of his head where the hatband had been. He looked...well not relaxed. Sort of tense, as if he were waiting for something. Like he had when they'd turned up the drive.

"Are you okay?" she asked.

He glared over at her. "What kind of question is that?"

She almost backed down but then decided he needed someone to force him to talk. "You look tense."

"You look sexy."

"Don't do that," she said. "I can tell something is up now that you're home and I just wanted to let you know I'm here if you want to talk."

He nodded. "This place doesn't feel like home to me."

She didn't understand that.

"Why not? I can tell you and your mom are close," she said.

"Yeah it's not her that I have the problem with."

"Who is it?"

"Boy, you home?" a loud booming voice called up the stairs.

She had her answer as she watched Gage's expression go completely neutral as he turned to open the door. "Yes, sir."

GAGE LEFT SIERRA in the guest room and went to the top of the stairs. He could tell by the way his father had called him *boy* that he knew it was Gage home and not Marty. This could be ugly. He turned back and noticed that Sierra had followed him into the hall.

"I brought a friend from Dallas, Dad. We'll come on down so you can meet her."

"Fine. I'll be on the porch with your Ma after I wash up."

He disappeared from the bottom of the stairs and Gage turned to Sierra. "I should have told you this before we got here, but my dad and I don't get along that great."

"You sort of mentioned it when you said that your relationship with him was complicated."

That's right. She had no idea about the other part. "Well, suffice it to say I've never lived up to his expectations. And then there is the Alzheimer's so there are times when he might say things that don't make any sense. He doesn't know you so I don't think you will have much trouble with that."

Her expression got sad and sympathetic. "Okay. I guess this is part of the reason why you were tense. Sorry for trying to grill you about it earlier."

He just shook his head. "It's fine. I didn't feel like you were pressuring me."

He started down the stairs and heard Sierra behind him. He could remember running down the stairs trying to beat Marty to the kitchen so he could get the best pancakes in the batch.

It was a like a punch to the gut when he was here. He missed his brother more. It was like this was where he felt his presence. When he climbed on a bull there were times that he felt like Marty was with him. That his ghost was watching over him, giving him some extra strength to hold on and keep his seat when he wasn't sure he could.

But here it was his brother and not the bull rider he felt. He hesitated on the last step, saw the dent in the wall that no amount of paint and plaster could fill in where he and Marty had been rough-housing and his brother had driven him into the wall.

He touched the indentation as he always did and then turned to see Sierra watching him. "Ma will make sure you have a good time while you're here."

She nodded. He didn't want to talk. He had too much going on inside his head and he needed to get away. But his father might be angry if he didn't show up on the back porch like he'd been told to. And then it could set him off. And Gage knew from a Skype call with his mom a few days ago that some of his dad's confusion was turning to violence.

"Let's go," he said.

He led the way past his father's den and then through the family room where Marty's and his trophies were displayed on a large bookcase. Sierra slowed down but Gage had no interest in looking at past glories so he kept walking. There was a small hallway that led to the kitchen and then out to the back porch.

His dad wasn't out there yet, he noted as he held the door for Sierra and let her walk past him. She smiled up at him and he realized whatever happened he was glad she was here with him.

There were six large rocking chairs that his mom had purchased at Cracker Barrel years ago. She kept them weatherproofed and had made some seat cushions for them in an all-weather canvas. He'd spent many a night out here after fighting with his dad, rocking and staring up at the night sky, wanting to get out of Oklahoma.

"Dad's home." He didn't know what else to say. This was what he'd been dreading but having Sierra by his side made it easier.

"I heard," his mom said, her voice flat. "You two take a seat. Can I get you some iced tea or lemonade?"

"Tea would be great," Sierra said.

"Same."

His mom got up to go inside and he and Sierra took a seat. Gage had no idea what to say. He didn't want to delve into his past history with his dad but honestly now that he'd agreed to let Sierra and Montez Denim shoot out here, he was beginning to think he shouldn't have.

"This is nice. I love living in downtown Dallas in my apartment but someday I think I'd like to have some land and a porch like this."

"Yeah?" he asked. "You don't seem the type."

"I've got some country roots you know. I'm not a total city slicker," she said. "The original Montez family were ranchers. That's why they started making jeans."

"I read the history when you sent me that press packet,"

he said.

"You did?"

"Yes. I know it probably seemed like I just signed the contract but I wanted to know what kind of people were sponsoring me."

"Good idea," she said. "But you know that the AEBR had already given us the go-ahead to sponsor the rookies. It's how they help build your name."

"Yeah, I know," he said. He'd been looking for an excuse to walk away from the tour before it even started. But he hadn't found it. There was so much about the AEBR that he liked for himself. And if he'd been doing it at eighteen he knew he'd love it. But at twenty-five with the pressure from his dad…it was different.

"THIS STEAK IS grilled exactly the way I like it," Sierra said to Gage's dad Lawton as the uncomfortable silence around the table grew.

"Probably the only time you'll get it that way if you stick with Gage," Lawton said. "He's not interested in learning the proper way of doing things."

"Now, Law, that's not true at all," Lucy said.

Gage didn't say a word—just sat next to her quietly cutting his meat. "I'd say that Gage knows the proper way to do a few things."

"Like what?"

"Bull riding," Sierra said. "He's at the top in points and there's a good chance he's going to win the tour."

Gage looked over at her. She shrugged. She wasn't going to sit here and listen to his dad malign him.

"He'll screw it up. Did he tell you he walked away from everything when he was eighteen? Had a big-time sponsorship deal and just walked out and never looked back," Lawton said.

"I didn't just walk away. There was more going on than that. Don't you remember?" Gage asked his father.

"It was a tough time," Lucy said. "I'm still not sure how I feel about my baby riding. But you know how stubborn a man can be once he sets his mind to something."

"I do, ma'am," Sierra said.

"Tell us more about Montez Denim. I know you will be filming here, right?"

"Yes. We want to show how our denim fits the western lifestyle—every part of it from the ranch, to the rodeo, to a night out on the town. We've sponsored the rookies. There are three from Brazil and two others who had enough points to ride this year. We're doing videos on the top three in points. Gage of course is number one."

"For now," Lawton grumbled. "And just so you know, he hasn't worked the ranch in years."

"Thank you, sir," Sierra said. "He's told me all about that and how he's been working on an oil rig in Scotland."

"Oil rig? Is that where you've been, boy?" his dad asked.

She glanced at Gage and he just nodded at his father. "Yes, sir. Remember Ma and I showed you those pictures of the North Atlantic."

His dad's brow furrowed. He just looked down at his plate and took another bite of the steak.

"Gage has promised me a property tour in the morning so I can find the best places to film," Sierra said. "Lucy, I do love these green beans with mushrooms. You must give me the recipe."

Though she didn't cook and had burned soup while microwaving it one time, she was determined to keep the conversation going. No matter what. She thought that dinner with both of her parents was bad. They'd divorced years ago but still fought like they were a couple. But it was a cakewalk compared to this.

"I will. It's one that my mama handed down to me," Lucy said. "I think I mentioned earlier that I have a pair of Montez Denim jeans that I love. I think I bought them twenty years ago."

"Danged woman will hang on to anything for a dog's age," Law said smiling over at Lucy and for the first time Sierra saw love in the older man's eyes.

"She sure will," Gage agreed. "Especially anger."

Lawton laughed and nodded. "We sure know that, don't we, boy?"

"Yes, sir."

The conversation turned to teasing Lucy about the things she held on to. Apparently, she had a bookshelf in the family room loaded up with cassette tapes she'd purchased in the '80s. Which turned the topic to music.

"In my opinion, there isn't a country singer today who can touch George Jones," Lawton said.

"I loved it when he sang with Tammy Wynette. Some of my favorite songs were recorded by those two. You know Tim McGraw and Faith Hill remind me of them—just not as tumultuous."

"That's for sure," Gage said. "On the rig, I listened to a lot of Big & Rich and Blake Shelton."

"I can't believe a son of mine lived and worked in a foreign country," Lawton said. "Did you like the music over there?"

"Yeah, it was okay," Gage answered. "Their steaks aren't as good as yours, sir."

His dad nodded. "Damned straight. Texas thinks they raise the best beef but they ain't got nothing on Oklahoma."

"Spoken like a man who makes his living off beef," Lucy said.

"I guess that makes me an expert," he said, winking at his wife. "Now word has it you made cobbler for dessert."

"I did," she said, getting up to clear her plate.

Sierra did the same, taking Gage's plate and her own and following Lucy into the kitchen.

She stood in the doorway for a second listening to the

dining room, but couldn't hear any conversation.

"Sorry about that. Those to have a tough relationship," Lucy said, scraping the plates and then putting them in dishwasher.

"It's okay. I just can't stand by and let him rip into Gage when I know he's really good at what he does."

"I saw that. I think you're good for him," Lucy said. "He's had too many years of just silently taking whatever his dad dished out."

"Why did he?"

"He's stubborn just like his pa. So, he's always just worked harder and done better at everything, waiting for Law to notice," Lucy said.

"But he never has," Sierra said. She could tell just by the way he'd spoken tonight. Everything Gage did wasn't quite good enough. "Was he the same with Marty?"

Lucy shook her head as she gathered dessert plates from the cabinet. "There's ice cream in the freezer and whipped cream in the fridge. Would you mind grabbing it?"

"Not at all," Sierra said, realizing she hadn't answered her question about Marty.

"Law and Marty had a special bond from the time he was born. I had hoped that maybe he and Gage would sort out their relationship once he was grown but Marty's death just made it all worse. Law said some things…well, that no man should ever say."

Sierra didn't need to hear anything else. She had a suspicion she could figure it out. Lucy dished up the dessert and put ice cream on two of them and whipped cream on one. "Which do you prefer?"

"Ice cream," she said.

"Just like Gage and me," Lucy said.

She knew it was silly but she liked that she had chosen the same as Gage and his mom. Sierra had the feeling that the close bond between mother and son was the one thing that had saved Gage all these years.

Chapter Twelve

"WANT TO GO for a ride? I'm not ready to turn in," Sierra said after they'd finished dessert and his dad had retired to his den and his mom had gone into the family room to watch one of her shows.

"Sure. I'm not too sure we should go on horseback. You aren't familiar with the terrain," he said. Hell, he probably wasn't either given that it had been a long time since he'd been home.

"That's fine. We could even walk or take your truck. Show me where you used to go when you needed space."

He rubbed his chin and thought about it. As soon as he could drive, which had been fourteen, he'd taken the ranch truck at night... "I've got an idea."

He took her hand, calling out to his mom that they'd be back later. She slid her fingers between his and held his hand loosely in hers. She smelled of summer even though it was waning and he remembered the way she'd defended him at dinner. He'd been surprised.

"Thanks for earlier with my dad."

She looked over at him. "You don't have to thank me. I

didn't say anything that wasn't true."

"I know. But you could have just kept quiet and you didn't."

"Well that's not my way."

His truck unlocked as they got close and he turned to look down at her. Her hair was loose again, brushing her shoulders, and the makeup she'd had on when they left Dallas had faded but she looked prettier now to him. He knew it was because he was starting to care for her.

And that should make alarm bells go off but it didn't. There was something about Sierra that just felt right. That made him want to believe he could be a better man.

Not that he was a bad man, but he'd always just felt disconnected from everyone and everything. She grounded him.

Danger.

He knew it. He had no idea how to make anything last. Not that she was asking for that. But damn, the way he felt about her was going to make letting her go hard.

"You're different than I expected," he said.

"Yeah? How?" she asked.

He opened the door and lifted her up onto the seat of the cab, remembering the last time he'd done so and what had happened afterward.

He stepped back. "You have strong opinions about different things than I expected you to.

"Like standing up for my friends?"

"Sort of. Just the way you are with your co-workers too:

fair but clearly the boss. And with me as my…what are we?"

"Friends."

"Friends…yes, we are," he said. He wanted it to be more. He wanted her to be his girlfriend but he wasn't that kind of guy. As always with Sierra he was reminded that he had these moments with her. Like getting on a bull each time the ride was short, exhilarating and temporary.

He got behind the wheel and started the engine without saying anything else. The radio came on to the satellite country station and they were playing an oldie by Willie Nelson.

Gage loved riding across the ranch with Sierra. It made him feel like he was really alive—something he rarely experienced away from the AEBR Tour.

It helped to take his mind off of the situation with his dad.

"Does your dad watch you ride?" she asked.

"Every time," he admitted.

"He does? I'm surprised he didn't praise you more tonight. I mean you're at the top in points. I think you could win the tour."

Tell her, he thought. Just casually throw out that when his dad watched him ride he thought that it was Marty. The only person who knew was his mom and she wasn't sure what to make of it either. And Gage could correct the old man but he never did.

"It's not his way," Gage said.

He could understand that and respect it. He knew that his father was always going to see him as the son who didn't measure up and maybe if Marty had lived that would have changed but the truth was, his brother hadn't lived and they were all playing the hands they'd been dealt. Him, his dad and his mom.

"I guess that makes sense," she said. He pulled to a stop on the top of a high ridge where they grazed the cattle in winter. The ridge was the best spot on the ranch for viewing the night sky. He turned off the engine and reached under the seat for the thick blanket that he kept there.

"Come on," he said.

"Where?"

"To the best planetarium in this part of the world."

There wasn't any light pollution from the city out here and as soon as his eyes adjusted to the darkness he could easily find his way.

Sierra had gotten out of the truck and walked over to him, her boots making a solid sound with each step she took. She was wearing a short-sleeved blouse that had a nipped-in waist, together with a pair of skintight Montez classic jeans.

He spread the blanket out and then sat down. Sierra did the same and he fell back looking up at the sky. She lay next to him, the sound of her breathing calming the last of the tension that had remained in him from dinner.

"I'm the worst at seeing any of the constellations. My dad used to take Savanna and me camping when we were little and he'd be like that's Sirius and that's the Big Dipper and Savanna could see it but honestly all I saw and still see are stars."

"I could point them out to you," he said. Sometimes when he'd been homesick he'd go out on the platform of the oil rig at night and look up at the sky and take comfort in seeing the constellations she'd named.

"Okay," she said.

He rolled over to his side and she did the same and they bumped heads. Not enough to really hurt but enough to make them both laugh.

"I'm so awkward," she said.

But she wasn't. Not really. He pulled her into his arms, forgetting about stars. He didn't want to gaze at constellations in the sky when he had a heavenly body right next to him.

And right now, he had this woman in his arms. A woman he'd been thinking about in inconvenient sexual terms since he'd met her.

"Do you want me, Sierra?" he asked her. "Even after my dad pointed out all of my flaws?"

She put her hand on his face. "He sees you through a broken glass."

Was that it? For a long time, he'd wondered if maybe the broken thing was inside of him.

"And I do want you very much."

He shifted around on the blanket until he was seated and

could pull her onto his lap. She straddled him, wrapping her arms around his shoulders, and then shifted around until she settled onto him.

"Comfortable?"

"Yes." She pushed back from him, putting one hand between them. "Gage?"

"Yes?"

"How about taking off your shirt?" Sierra asked.

He arched one eyebrow at her, but did as she asked. Unsnapping the pearl buttons on his western shirt and shrugging out of it. "You seem to have a thing about me without a shirt."

"Yes, I do."

Her hands on his shoulders were light and she rubbed them back and forth over him, one hand drifting down his chest, her fingers rubbing over his pectorals and then lower. He shivered under her touch, wanting this moment to last forever but knowing that he needed more. He needed Sierra in a way that scared him more than getting on the back of a bull. And the only time he felt like she was really, truly his was when he was buried deep inside of her.

He wanted to be chill and act like this wasn't a big deal to him but when Sierra touched him he didn't feel like he was filling in for someone else. She was making love with him. She didn't see the specter of another lover and that made him...well, hell, it made him feel too much. And emotions had never led him to anything but destruction.

She lowered her hand to his erection, running over its length. "I guess you like that."

He had to focus on this moment, stop feeling anything except her limbs entwined with his. Her body against his. Her lips under his.

"Darlin', I love it," he said, pulling her to him. He lifted her slightly so she was pressed against him from chest to hips.

"But not as much as I enjoy touching you," he said, sweeping his hands down her torso. She was soft, her skin so smooth...perfect. Unlike him she seemed to have no flaws inside or out.

He sucked her lower lip into his mouth as he shifted his shoulders against her, rubbing his torso against her full breasts.

"That's nice," she said.

Blood roared in his ears and he felt that shiver of sensation down his spine. He was hard and aching and needed to be inside her. Now.

Impatient with the fabric of her clothing and he shoved her shirt out of his way and undid her pants. "Stand up and take those pants off."

She did as he asked, working her boots off and then those jeans. He loved the way she swiveled her hips as she pushed the denim down her legs. He was so busy watching her he realized he was still wearing his jeans. He pushed his off and then reached for the condom he'd put in his back pocket earlier, before they left the house.

He pulled her back onto his lap. Her legs parted and her thighs rubbed against his, as she shifted around finding the right position. The tip of his hard-on brushed against her center.

She was warm and wet. He slipped one finger under the material of her underwear. Their eyes met when she sighed and he knew that something was changing between them. This was more than sex.

Her eyelids dropped as she arched her back and took him deeper into her body. Her lips were parted and her hair fell down over her face and his hips jerked forward. He had to look away to keep from losing himself at that moment.

He pulled her head down and tasted her mouth. Her lips parted under his and he thrust his tongue deep into her mouth. His cock was buried deep inside of her and he wanted to take her so deeply that they'd never be able to be two separate people again.

He caressed her spine. She felt so delicate in his arms as he ran his hand down her back to the indentation above her backside.

She moaned, which set fire to him, and he knew that no matter how long he wanted this to last, he had no control where Sierra was concerned. He pushed her back so he could see her better. Every time he saw her naked he was hit with a bolt of desire that burned through the bull of regular life and made it seem as if there was nothing more important than holding Sierra and making love to her.

He rested a hand on the small of her back. She closed her

eyes, her hips undulating, and when he touched her nipples gooseflesh spread down over her chest toward her belly button.

He took a deep breath and then ran his finger between her breasts, the backs of his fingers brushing the sides of her breasts.

He varied his thrusts, finding a rhythm that would draw out the tension gathering inside of him—not unlike how he felt when he was on the back of a bull and he was about to leave the chute. Excitement, anticipation and the more times he made love to her a hint of danger. Because this was Sierra and not just a casual lay.

He held her hips to him to give him deeper access to her body. He lost control thrusting harder and deeper until he yelled her name as he came. Then he cradled her to his chest and just held her like he'd never have to let her go. A bull rider's life was rough and tumbled. Could be short as Marty had proven—and Gage had seen too many riders who were beat-up and old before their time.

He wanted more for Sierra and he wondered if he dared to let himself believe he deserved more for himself. Imagined he somehow could have Sierra not just for the length of the tour the way some of the riders treated the buckle bunnies, but for the rest of his life. Because as she kissed his shoulder and wrapped her arms around him, holding him, he knew he never wanted to let her go.

She shivered and he reached for his shirt, draping it over her back, because he wasn't ready to stop holding her.

Chapter Thirteen

SOMETHING HAD CHANGED between them after the night they made love under the stars. They had filmed the promo they needed and Gage had left for Lubbock. She'd headed home to Dallas but he texted her all the time and they'd had a few video calls.

She missed him and she could no longer deny that she loved him. At first it was easy to say it was simply a crush or something she would get over after they'd slept together, but she knew now that wasn't the case.

He'd done well in Lubbock—still up at the top in points—and she knew he was traveling to Shreveport, which wasn't too far from Dallas. Well, three hours. She'd waited for Gage to suggest that he stop by and see her on his way to Shreveport but he hadn't.

She had never been one to wait so she sent an email to her assistant informing him she'd need a room in Shreveport for the weekend. And he popped into her office.

"I thought you were done with the AEBR Tour and weren't going to any more stops," he said.

"I changed my mind," she said.

"You changed it or that tall, drink of water, Gage Powell, did?" he asked.

"Stop it," she said. "I was going to see if the fans are responding to the new campaign. But I've changed my mind."

Now that she'd said it out loud she felt foolish. She was chasing him again. He'd left her in Sacramento and she knew he was on tour and trying to put in his best rides each week. He had been texting and calling her but she wanted to see him. Didn't he want to see her?

"Okay, if that's what you want, but if you want to go you know I won't judge," he said.

"I know. I've made up my mind to go," she said. "But I hate to feel like I'm running after him. You know?"

He came in and closed the door and then sat down in one of the guest chairs. "I'm going to tell you something I haven't told anyone else. When Shaun and I were first dating he thought I was a big flirt."

"You are a big flirt."

"Do you want to hear this or not?"

"Yes."

"So we had this one incredible night together and then he didn't call. And I was like fine whatever at first, but I couldn't stop thinking about him and so I went to his work and just watched him from the parking lot—like a creepy stalker! But it wasn't creepy. I had missed him. Just seeing him made me realize that I needed to call him again."

"And you did."

"No, because I was afraid. It took me three months to call him and by that time I was afraid he'd have forgotten me, but he hadn't. Fear robbed me of those three months, Sierra. Don't let fear rob you of anything."

She sat back in her chair and rocked it back and forth. "It's so hard, caring about someone else. I mean there's no guarantee that the other person even likes you back. He's driving close enough to Dallas that we could meet up and he didn't suggest it."

"You'll only regret it if you don't go after him," Marcos said. "Love is scary and exhilarating and the best damned thing you can experience. But you have to commit to it one hundred percent."

She thought about what her assistant said. Had she been hedging her bets? Heck, of course she was. There wasn't a single member of her immediate family who had any luck with romance and love. They were all serial daters who never found something solid. And Sierra had always craved that stability.

"Okay. Book it and give me a few extra days there."

"Yes! You won't regret it," he said, coming around her desk to give her a hug before leaving the office.

She hoped she wouldn't regret it but she knew she had to go and try. Maybe he'd been waiting for a signal from her that she wanted to see him. Maybe he was afraid to be the one to admit to feeling something for her.

Gage was in a tense situation, trying to stay at the top of

the points so he could keep his dad proud of him. And though Lawton had been hard on Gage at dinner, she'd seen that he cared for him too. When they'd teased Lucy about her music. It was only when Lawton compared Gage to Marty that he got a little ornery.

She sent an email to her dad, telling him her plans to be in Shreveport and he sent back a thumbs-up emoji. Her father had taken to emojis in a big way. He said if it were possible to just communicate with emojis and emoticons he'd be a happy man.

She sent him back the kissy face and then started packing up to head home. Marcos sent her hotel reservation to her smart phone and the directions to the hotel in Shreveport to her maps app as well.

She left her office and he looked up. "Don't worry. It's going to work out."

"How do you know?"

"I saw the way he looked at you when we all went to dinner," Marcos said.

"How did he look at me?" she asked.

"Like he was fascinated by you," he said. "And trust me that's a good thing."

She nodded and then hugged him before leaving the office. Fascinated by her. She hoped that Marcos was right. She'd never done anything this scary. She couldn't remember the last time she was this nervous. There were so many things that could go wrong. She might disrupt his ride or mess with his juju and she didn't want to do that.

But another part of her was just excited at the thought of seeing him again. Touching him again and being in the same city as him.

GAGE HADN'T EXPECTED to see Sierra waiting when he came out of the locker room, but there she was. Wearing a denim skirt that hugged her hips and ended just above her knees paired with a cute little blouse and a pair of flat shoes. She was leaning against the wall and had been looking down at her cell phone until he walked into the hall.

"Hi there."

"Hey. I didn't know you were going to be here," he said. She was a sight for sore eyes. He'd missed her more than he wanted to admit and he wasn't having the best day. His mom had called earlier to tell him his dad had fallen off the Mule—a four-wheel drive vehicle they used on the ranch—and hit his head pretty hard. They were in the ER waiting to find out if he had a concussion.

"It was a last-minute thing," she said. "Want to go grab dinner?"

She stood there all stiff and unsure and he wasn't up to reading any subtle clues tonight. She was here. He needed someone who cared for him and she was here.

"I'd love to. Man, I missed you," he said, drawing her

into his arms and kissing her.

"Me too. That's why I'm here," she said. "So how'd you do in qualifying?"

"Not bad," he said. "Dad had a fall at the ranch. I'm waiting to hear if he did any damage. Mom said he hit his head and then joked that we know how hard that is so he should be okay."

"Well he does have a hard head, but I can tell you're concerned. Is there anything I can do?" she asked.

"No. Let's get dinner. I mean it's not like Dad and I are close," he said.

"But you are," Sierra pointed out. "You both tease your mom."

"That's not really anything," Gage said.

"I think it is," she said. "I can see that when he measures you and Marty together he's completely irrational but when he forgets it's easy to tell that he sees you differently."

It was nice that she thought so but Gage knew his dad had backed down because he could tell Sierra was going to keep defending him. They had never really gotten on when it was just the two of them.

It didn't stop him from loving the old man but he knew that their relationship was broken and the knock to the head might mean that Gage was running out of time to fix it.

He drove to one of the casinos in Shreveport that had a pretty good steak restaurant. Sierra made light conversation the entire way, telling him how good the new ads were doing and how consumers were really responding to them. They got to the restaurant and gave their names to the waitress.

"I'm glad. Hope I don't lose and screw things up," he said.

"What? Don't say anything like that. The consumers and the fans like you, Gage. It's an added bonus that you're winning but they are responding to you," she said.

"Sorry. I'm in a pissy mood today, darlin'," Gage said.

"Is it just your dad?" she asked.

He shrugged. "I have to make a decision about next year too. I started the AEBR Tour because I thought it would be for a year. Now I'm liking it and I'm doing good. But I've seen some of the guys who've been doing it since they were eighteen and this life takes a toll on a guy."

"It does. I've seen it too through the rookies we sponsor each year. The ones who stay on and the ones who move on or choose another life," Sierra said. "What do you want to do?"

"That's the million-dollar question, isn't it?" Gage asked. He signaled the waitress for more sweet tea. He didn't have an answer for Sierra. Part of his decision was based on his parents. Would his dad even know if he rode again next year? Another part of him was concerned about his relationship with Sierra. He hadn't been lying when he said he missed her. A part of him wanted to come home to her every night, but that wasn't possible. He didn't have any normal job skills. So he could either go back to the oil company or stay here and ride.

Neither solution was going to work for the two of them.

"Gage?"

"Yeah?" he asked.

She didn't say anything so he looked up and saw she'd rested her elbows on the table and leaned forward to watch him. She had her hair twisted up, which made her features look even more delicate than they usually did. She was too soft for him. She needed a guy who knew what he wanted. So, what did he want?

Her.

"The only thing I know right now, Sierra, is I want to be with you. I don't know how that will work out and I can't think about it until after the finals in Fort Worth."

"That's all right by me," she said.

"Really?" he asked. He'd expected her to want more details from him.

"Yes," she said, smiling at him. "That's what I want too. I came here because texts and calls weren't enough. I needed to see you and touch you."

She was saying exactly what he'd been thinking and feeling. And he realized as he listened to her talk that he loved her. He who'd never said those words to anyone but his mother was in love with Sierra Montez. Denim heiress and sophisticated lady.

Don't screw it up.

He heard Marty's voice in his mind. And mentally

shoved that voice down deep inside of him. He might not know what was next for him with his career or if his father would ever look at him and see the man he'd become. But he did know he wanted Sierra in his life and she wanted him in hers.

SIERRA HADN'T REALIZED how much had changed since Sacramento but as she stood in the VIP section and saw Gage get in the chute and onto the bull she felt nauseous. She had watched him ride so many times but then had avoided it since they'd become lovers. She'd thought it was simply because she wanted to keep from feeling regret at first and then after their time in Oklahoma from missing him but she saw now that she couldn't stomach watching him ride.

She knew he was good.

That a clean, hard ride was what he was known for and he'd stick, he always did, but she was so nervous her hands started shaking. She turned just as the gate opened and the crowded roared as the bull entered the arena: 1,700 pounds of bucking bull and Gage was on his back. Except Gage wasn't doing what he normally did.

Horrified she watched as he lost his seat and was tossed off of the back of the bull. She saw him wrenching his hand trying to get free of the rope. The rodeo clown rushed into the arena and Sierra wanted to turn away but she couldn't.

Finally, they got him free but he had taken a beating before they did.

The announcer was making some chatter to distract the crowd but there was a buzzing in Sierra's ears as she fought her way out of the VIP stand down to sports medicine. He had been helped out of the arena and that was the last she saw.

She stopped at the bottom of the stairs, hugging her waist and bending over to clear the stars from her eyes.

She loved Gage.

And he'd almost been trampled to death doing his job. This was the life he'd been talking about last night.

He was in the points, in the money, and next year expectations were that he'd do even better. He'd made a name for himself and she didn't want to stand in his way, but there was no way she could endure this.

She would stay away, she thought. She could do that. He'd have to ride next year especially if he was injured. She knew the way athletes' minds worked. Gage would want to repeat his success to prove to himself that he was as good as this season had shown him to be. And she was going to have to watch.

"Are you okay?"

She looked up to see a stranger standing there watching her.

She nodded. "I'm good. Thanks."

She was fine. It was Gage who might be seriously injured. She hurried away from the stands into the private corridor that led to the changing rooms and the sports medicine area. She flashed her VIP credentials and kept on walking. She needed to see him.

To make sure he was okay. She could only concentrate on this moment, on the now. She'd figure out what was going to happen next between them later. When she got to the door where the medical room was, she hesitated again when she heard some cursing from behind the door.

She knocked on it and then opened it up. Gage was white and there was dirt and blood all over his face and torso. His shirt was torn and he looked up as she entered and she'd never seen him look angry or less than approachable.

"Sorry. I just needed to see if you were okay," she said.

"I'm fine," he grunted.

The physician, Doc Freeman, glanced over at Gage and then back at her. "She can stay if you want or she can wait outside."

"Outside," Gage said.

Sierra nodded and backed out of the room. She felt small and embarrassed that he hadn't wanted her there. And she thought back to what Marcos had said. That love was a gamble. Last night she felt like she'd been dealt a winner hand and was riding a winning streak. Now she was just standing in the hall like a buckle bunny who didn't have the good sense to realize what she was.

She knew she was overreacting, that it was a residual reaction to seeing him injured and not being able go and hold him and reassure herself that he was okay.

But if he'd smiled at her... What the heck did she expect? He'd been bounced on the arena floor.

She was overreacting.

"Sierra?"

Her sister was coming down the hall toward her, her dark hair flying around her face, and she pulled Sierra into a bear hug as soon as she was close enough.

"This is the guy? Gage Powell? You've been so secretive," Savanna said.

Sierra just hugged her big sister back. "Yes. I didn't want to talk about it."

"You don't have to. I'm right here with you. He'll be okay. That wasn't the worst we've seen."

"I know," Sierra said. Her sister stood next to her until the door opened and Gage came out. He was cleaned up and through his torn shirt she could see his ribs had been wrapped and it looked like his shoulder too. He had a bandage on his forehead and he smelled of antiseptic and sweat.

Savanna squeezed her hand and then walked down the hall to give them some privacy.

Sierra hesitated. He took a ginger step toward her and she went to his side. "You scared me."

"Sorry."

She put her arm around him and led him down the hall

toward the changing area where the showers were. "Are you okay?"

"Yeah. Listen I'm going to be a while. I'll meet you at the Montez Denim fan zone later, okay?"

She hesitated. Something wasn't right. Something had changed.

"Gage—"

"Don't. I don't want to talk right now. I think I might say something I'll regret. Just meet me later."

She nodded and watched him limp away from her. Her heartbeat was so strong she could hear it in her ears and she wondered if this time when he walked away it was goodbye.

It felt like it.

Chapter Fourteen

S IERRA DIDN'T SEE Gage until the events were finished and most of the riders and all of the fans had cleared out. She'd stayed until there wasn't a soul left at the fan zone. He wasn't coming. Her gut had told her that earlier as she'd stood there watching the throngs of fans and riders mingling. Everyone was there. Everyone except Gage.

Her sister had taken off with her current beau but said to text her if Sierra needed her. She wasn't sure what Savanna thought she could do.

Could she make Gage love her?

Could she make him realize that they should be together?

Somehow, she doubted that was what her sister had in mind.

She finally went to his truck and waited for twenty minutes before he came walking toward her. She remembered what Marcos had said about lost months but right now turning tail and leaving sounded better to her than facing him. He'd been the one who'd taken a beaten from a huge, raging beast but she was the one who felt battered.

Her heart wasn't going to be whole if this didn't work

out the way she wanted it to.

His normal gait was slow and he had a hitch in it. He looked rough and tough. And despite the battering he'd taken there was an aura of danger around him.

She bit her lower lip and knew she needed to just be cool. He'd had a rough day and a rougher night. He'd been worried about his dad before he'd ridden. The last thing he needed was for her to lose her cool.

But she'd never been in love before and she had thought after last night that things would be different between them.

"Sierra."

Just the way he'd said her name made her realize that this wasn't going to be a conversation she'd enjoy. In fact, she was pretty damned sure that it was going to end with her in tears.

"Gage."

He sighed. "I'm in a lot of pain and not really up for this conversation."

She just stood there. She wasn't one to back down and he knew it. "What conversation? Because I don't see that anything has changed since this morning when you told me that you wanted to figure out how to make things work."

He shook his head.

"Everything changed, darlin'. I could have died. You know that's what happened with Marty and while I was being tossed around like a ragdoll that's all that was going through my head. Except Marty had been smart enough not to be involved with anyone."

"I don't know that was smart," Sierra said. "That ride didn't change how I feel about you."

"Well it changed something in me," he said.

"What? What could it have possibly changed?"

"I'm doing this for my dad. And until you showed up I've been sticking each ride and hanging on with no problems. You are a distraction, Sierra, and one I don't need," he said.

"A distraction?" she asked, trying to be cool but it was getting harder.

"Yeah. And I stayed up too late last night having sex when I should have been sleeping," he said.

"I didn't make you have sex with me, Gage Powell. In fact, you rode pretty damned good in Sacramento and we were up way later that night."

"Well, I didn't care about you then, so you weren't in my head the next morning."

"Shouldn't that mean something? You care about me and I care about you. I don't want this to end."

"Well that's not the way this works. We have to both think it can work and I'm not sure it can."

She saw that his eyes were bloodshot and as he got closer she noticed how tired and beaten he looked, but he was also determined. She stopped standing by his truck and went to his side. She wanted this to work and she needed to be all in.

She wrapped her arm around him carefully, looking up

at him.

"I love you," she said, putting all of her emotions into those words. No more hiding and pretending. "I haven't said that to many people. Just my sister and parents. And I wasn't looking for love or even looking for you, but it happened and I don't want to let you slip away."

"Ah, dammit, darlin'. I love you too. In fact, I love you too much to put you through this. Today just brought home the reality of what I've been doing. I love riding. I don't think I can quit. And I said it was for my daddy that I was doing it but that was a lie. A big ol' selfish lie. I'm doing it for me."

"That's fine. We'll figure it out. I can go on the road with the tour. You know I run the sponsor program," she said.

But he shook his head. "That's not possible. I know what it's like to watch someone you love die, darlin'. I'm not about to do that to you."

"You're not going to die."

"You don't know that," he said.

"I do. We got this," she said. "You and me together make a formidable team. Give us a chance."

He leaned down, resting his forehead on the top of her head, and she held him. But even as she did she knew that her hold on him was tenuous.

"You can take the next few months to figure it out. You have enough points to qualify for next year and won't have to decide anything until December."

"Sierra, I'm riding next week in Little Rock."

"You can barely stand up."

"So. I'll be fine. I'm taped up good."

"At least skip Little Rock," she said. "Wait for Nashville."

"I can't. Dad's coming to see me ride in Little Rock."

"He might not even know it's you," Sierra said. "Be sensible."

"I'm not discussing this," he said. "I started this for Dad and no matter what it's turned into, he's planning to be in Little Rock and I'm going to have a good clean ride."

"That's foolish. That's pride."

He didn't say anything and she realized she wasn't going to change his mind. She knew from being around the tour for as long as she had been that his injuries were serious. The head wound probably meant a concussion. And he wasn't even going to think about taking a week off.

"What if you don't pass medical?"

"I will," he assured her.

"What if I asked you not to ride?"

"The answer would be no."

"You're an idiot," she said. "Riding isn't going to make your dad love you. He's never going to look at you and see whatever it was he thought he saw in Marty. Why are you doing this?"

"I don't reckon that's any of your damn business, Sierra,"

he said, walking past her and getting in his truck.

She knew she'd said too much but had no way to take back the words. She wasn't even sure she would if she could. She didn't want to see him do something stupid that wasn't going to help him get what he wanted and needed from his dad.

Or from her.

She shook her head and walked away from him.

SIERRA HAD STUBBORNLY refused to go back home to Dallas even though Gage had done everything in his power to force her. Instead she'd followed him in her rental car to Little Rock. She'd parked in the sponsor lot when they got to the arena and he pretended he hadn't watched in his rearview mirror until she got out of the car and walked toward the Montez Denim tent.

Fuck.

He ached. There wasn't a part of his body that didn't hurt and suddenly he knew why most riders retired long before thirty. How many years could a body take this kind of abuse? He had started this year to prove something. He'd pretended it was something for his dad or for himself or even for Marty but now he wasn't sure what it was exactly that he was here for.

He wasn't questioning his purpose. He was neck and

neck with Kane. He couldn't miss riding for a week. He might lose. He'd forfeit his shot at the gold buckle and he just wasn't sure he could do it.

It was the one thing that he'd have that Marty had never achieved. Could never achieve.

He felt small and petty but there it was. He wasn't walking away from riding again. He was a damned good rider. He'd thought all those years ago that he'd been doing it for his dad but it turned out that he'd really done it for himself.

He saw the other riders pull in and make their way to the locker room. It was time to soak his old bones and he was going to have convince Doc Freeman that he could ride. That wouldn't be hard. Doc got that all of them were here for a reason. No one did this for the fun of it. Or if they did, not for long.

His phone pinged and he glanced down to see a message from Sierra. His heart beat a little bit faster.

Sierra: *Your folks are here at the fan zone.*

Gage: *Thanks. I'll be over shortly.*

The message window had dancing dots and he waited to see what she was typing to respond but then just a thumbs-up icon appeared. What had she been about to say?

And why did it matter?

He'd kicked her when he'd been down. He'd driven her away. The way he did with anyone he cared for. He was being treated the way he deserved.

He scrubbed his hand over his face and realized he was on edge. He got out of the truck, kicked the front tire as hard as he could and felt a bolt of pain shoot up his leg.

"You okay?"

Glancing over his shoulder he saw Kane standing there with his gear in one hand, his hat in the other. Of course, his rival would see him making an ass of himself. Though Kane was more than just a rider on the tour. They'd become friends of a sort.

"Yeah. Just wishing I could kick my own ass," Gage admitted.

Kane laughed.

"After qualifying I'm willing to oblige," Kane said.

"Hopefully I'll draw a bull that will take the rage that's in me," Gage said. "But thanks for the offer."

"Any time."

Kane walked toward the arena and Gage locked the doors to the cab of his truck and walked over toward the fan zone. As soon as he entered the main fan area he was stopped by fans. He posed for selfies, signed Montez Denim posters and even signed one woman's bosom.

He felt someone watching him and glanced up to see Sierra watching him. She looked older than he'd seen her look before. She had her hair pulled back tight in some sort of high updo and wore a pants suit that made her look ten years older than he knew her to be. There were faint lines under her eyes and he realized it was because of him. That was what he'd done to her. He could have left her with a smile.

But instead he'd kept coming back, trying to take something for himself. Trying to pretend he wasn't the portent of destruction that he'd always been, thinking he could pay the price, but instead it was Sierra who was paying it.

He hadn't wanted that.

He turned away from her, but then knew he had to apologize.

"Sorry," he mouthed to her.

She nodded. Then wrapped one arm around her waist and pointed to a table where his parents were seated and waiting for him. When he glanced back to her, Sierra was gone.

He knew it was only fitting but he missed her. He could pretend that by ignoring his feelings they weren't real but he knew he loved her.

And that love meant he had to be a better man.

SIERRA HURRIED BACK past the temporary tattoo station and into the back where they stored the posters for each of the riders. She crouched down behind one of the large boxes, pulled her knees to her chest, buried her face against them and cried.

He'd signed some skank's chest like…like it was nothing.

What did she expect? Well, certainly not to see him smile down at the woman and then meet her gaze without a hint of shame. She had to stop this.

She had to stop following him around like some sort of lost puppy dog.

She'd been around the tour long enough to know that a rider as high in the points as Gage was never going to skip a ride. But all of that went out of her mind when it came to Gage. She knew it was because she loved him and despite everything she knew she still did.

Well she wasn't fickle so it wasn't surprising that during the last week she hadn't fallen out of love with him. But she'd wanted to see something in him. Something that would show her he was sorry for what had happened, but that wasn't his way.

She'd thought…she'd thought now that she was older she would know herself. Know her heart well enough to take a gamble and actually win at love, but it seemed that she was a Montez through and through. There wasn't a happily ever after in the stars for her.

The flap opened and Savanna walked in. Sierra sat as quietly as she could, hoping her sister didn't see her. And at first Savanna was busy tapping furiously on her phone, typing out a message. Then she put the phone down on the stack of boxes that Sierra was sitting behind and started to adjust her breasts in the low-fitting top when their eyes met.

"Sierra? What are you doing in here?" Savanna asked.

"What does it look like?"

"Oh, honey," Savanna said, dropping down to sit next to her. "It gets easier."

"What does?"

"This life. Falling for a rider. They are tough. You know that it's all about sticking the ride, getting enough points and winning the buckle. We're just a distraction when they need it and when they don't they move on."

Sierra's heart ached. Not for herself because she wasn't going to do this again, but for Savanna who had done this year after year. "I'm not ever getting involved with a rider again."

"You say that now, but next year, there will someone who'll catch your eye," Savanna said. "That's what always happens to me. And now I'm getting older and am less of a novelty...some days I wonder how my life became this."

She reached over and patted her sister's shoulder. She got it. She really did. "You like it."

"Not right now," she said. "The Brazilian I've been see-ing has a fiancée and she's coming to the finals so he said we should cool things off starting now."

"That's still a few weeks away," she said. She was very aware of when Gage would take his last ride and his contract with Montez Denim would be up. And he'd walk away.

"He said he wanted to keep himself for her when she ar-rived so he'd be hungry."

Suddenly Sierra felt sorry for her sister. She knew that

Savanna would scoff if she tried to comfort her.

"Men."

Savanna smiled. "What's going on with you and Gage?"

"Nothing. He doesn't need to be distracted by a girl. He has his own agenda and I don't have a place in it."

"Are you sure?"

She thought of that moment when their eyes met and she'd seen his demons in his gaze. She'd wanted to go to him and pull him into her arms, but he'd just mouthed the word sorry. Was that even a proper apology?

It was his way of making something better in his mind.

"Yeah. Damn, I'm dumb. Looking at me sitting behind the posters, crying like a baby. I can't do this," Sierra said. She pushed herself to her feet.

She rubbed her hands over her face and then reached up taking the elastic from the tight bun she'd twisted it into this morning. She shook her head and then took her own phone and used the front-facing mirror to check herself out. She still looked tired and drained. She forced a smile.

"Me either. Enough feeling sorry for myself. I'm a Montez."

"That's right the Montez girls aren't going to hide out," Sierra added.

Savanna smiled at her and then linked her arm through Sierra's as they went back out into the main fan area. Gage's dad was talking loudly about how his son was going to win it all.

For a moment Sierra wondered if he knew it was Gage riding and not Marty. But that no longer mattered. Gage had made it clear he didn't want or need him in his life. She saw Lucy standing off to one side watching both of her men. She had that mixture of pain and pride in her eyes and Sierra realized that she'd come to care for much more than just Gage.

She went over to Lucy.

"I'm so glad you guys were able to come to Little Rock," Sierra said.

"Me too. It's so nice to see Gage's picture everywhere and the fans who are waiting to see him. I never realized it was this big. I figured a few people knew his name, but nothing like this."

"We are very happy with our partnership with him. Gage is a really good rider."

Lucy turned to her. "It's more than a business deal, isn't it? I had the feeling when you were both at the ranch that there was more between you."

"Not anymore," Sierra said.

"I'm…I don't know what to say. I thought you were different and I liked seeing you with him."

Sierra had too but she wasn't going to force it. He said to give him space and he didn't need her and she had her pride. She'd gone to him once, but how many times was she supposed to do that?

"I think you have your VIP credentials for the weekend,"

Sierra said. "If you need anything else just let any Montez Denim staff member know and we will take care of it for you."

"Where will you be?" Lucy asked.

"Back in Dallas. I have some stuff to take care of for the finals in Fort Worth," Sierra said. Like sorting out her life and trying to figure out how to see Gage and not feel that mix of love, fear and anger.

She walked away from the fan event and out of the arena. She texted Savanna to let her know what was going on and then just got in her car and sat there. She couldn't run away. The finals were coming up. A million dollars was on the line and Gage was going to ride. She told herself she was staying because she was a sponsor and needed to make sure she had the PR campaign ready to go but she knew she was here for Gage.

No matter how she might wish otherwise.

Chapter Fifteen

THE AEBR ROLLED into Fort Worth and took over the town. Sierra had almost booked a vacation out of town but she wasn't up to trying to explain that to her father so instead she was here at the ballroom in the hotel watching the riders dressed in their Sunday best mingling with the high-paying fans, sponsors and other folks associated with the tour.

This was the last ride of the year. There was a buzz of excitement that hadn't been there since the first ride of the tour. Everyone was excited. Kane and Gage were close in the points and their rides on Friday and Saturday night would determine the winner. The Thursday night party served two functions. One was to kick off the finals and the other was to give everyone a chance to hang out together before they went home. Back to their ordinary lives away from the tour.

Savanna had hooked up with an old beau and was out on the dance floor with him. Though every time that Sierra looked at her sister, she noticed she was watching the Brazilian she'd been sleeping with during the tour.

She hoped she never looked at Gage the way her sister

was watching her former lover. There was a tinge of bitterness in her gaze.

"Sierra."

She turned around, saw him standing there in a pair of dark wash Montez Denim jeans, his hand-tooled Kelly Boots and a denim shirt that was decorated on the shoulders and had those fancy pearl snap-buttons down the front. He held his black Stetson loosely in one hand and stood there watching her.

"Gage. I heard you did well in Little Rock and in Nashville."

"I did all right," he said. "Kane and I are so close we can both feel it."

"I noticed that. How's your dad doing?" she asked.

Small talk. She could do this. Just keep talking until someone came along who she could use to get away from him. But he looked so good. He'd healed up from his injuries. She'd heard that via the grapevine. And there was something more settled about him than there had been before.

"He has his good days and his bad ones. They are here," he said. "Both of them wanted to see me ride."

"You or Marty?" she asked. Then regretted her cattiness. "I'm sorry. I thought I could be cool and act like you are just another rider to me, but you're not."

She pivoted on her heel and walked away from him. What had she been thinking?

She felt his hand on her arm, drawing her to a stop.

"Don't walk away like that. I'm so tired of watching you leave me."

"I didn't leave you. Not really."

"You did," he said. "I know I was an ass and deserved it but please don't walk away again."

"I don't know how to stay. I don't know what you want from me," she said.

"I don't know either," he admitted.

She nodded.

He just stood there and finally she knew she'd have to make the first move, but she had no idea what that would achieve. Another hot hotel hookup. More sharing her soul and having him bare his own before he backed away.

"I have to go," she said. "Good luck when you ride tomorrow."

She turned and this time when she wanted to feel his hand on her arm there was nothing. She left the hotel and when she got outside she tipped her head up to the sky and took a deep breath. The stars were the only witness to her tears as she climbed into her car and drove back to Dallas.

GAGE WAS IN the dressing room in Fort Worth on Saturday, checking his rope and working over it. Nicholas Blue had come to see him ride since they were in Dallas and he'd brought his wife, Reba, and their toddler daughter Martina: his goddaughter who they'd named after Marty.

Nick—a former bull rider himself—was going to spot him in the chute. But he had time. He had his father's knife, the one he gave him when he'd been home visiting with Sierra, so he could trim off any frayed bits of rope.

He kept his eyes down on his hands and the rope so he wouldn't be tempted to go back out and look up in the stands. She wasn't there. He knew she wasn't. She'd made it clear that she wouldn't watch him ride and he got it. Hell, no he didn't.

This was it. He had to stick tonight. His last ride of the year. He wanted to do it for Marty and for his dad, he thought.

"Gage?"

"Huh?"

"I asked if you were ready for your ride," Kane said. They were both loners and God knew the two of them were rivals...hell, they all were. There wasn't any one of them on the tour who didn't want to win. But he and Kane had bonded over the last few events. There was something about the life that sort of got to Gage as they neared the end of the tour.

"Yeah, sorry. Distracted."

"That's not like you," Kane said.

"It's not. That knock I took in Shreveport must have rattled my senses. My daddy always did say I couldn't afford too many hits to the head."

Kane laughed and shook his head. "Truer words have never been spoken."

Gage adjusted the rope and then slowly tuned everything out. Sierra and her worries about him riding while he was still a little bit injured. His mom who'd warned him that this mission he was on wasn't going to bring him the closure he craved. And his dad who looked at him like he hung the moon all the while thinking he was his dead brother.

He shoved all three of them firmly out of his mind and thought about Marty. This ride was for his brother and it was for Gage. He felt connected to Marty now.

Kane left and Gage looked back at the rope, which didn't need any more attention. He had come here to prove something but he had to admit he'd found he liked the tour. Bull riding had never been something he did for himself and he hadn't even realized it until Sierra had pointed it out.

Of course, he knew he shouldn't have lost his temper the way he had. He always did say things he didn't mean. Things meant to hurt. And from the look in her eyes when she'd walked away he'd done a good job at it.

Regret was a familiar mantle and he wore it as he always did. He couldn't help but notice that he was too much like his father. He'd always wanted the old man to see him and to prove he was better than Marty, but the truth was he'd spent too much time watching the old man and had picked up his habits.

"Hey, Gage. Finally got the girls settled. Martina is looking forward to seeing you ride. It took a lot of convincing for her to stay with Reba instead of coming down her to help her favorite Unca."

"I hope I can give her a ride worth watching," Gage said.

Nick quirked one eyebrow at him. "You okay?"

"Yeah, why?"

"Heard you took a rough tumble a few weeks ago," Nick said.

"I'm fine."

Nick put his hands up. "You don't have to convince me."

"I know," Gage said, glancing around the dressing room, which was pretty sparsely populated at the moment. "Sierra didn't want me to ride."

"She's the girl?"

"She's more than a girl, Nick. She's funny and feisty and everything I never knew I wanted and she asked me to sit out for a week…but I couldn't."

"Why not? Is the tour that important to you?" Nick asked. "I know you want to honor Marty's memory but—"

"It's not that. When Dad watches me ride, he thinks I'm Marty."

There, he'd said it. Told someone other than the women about this thing he'd been doing.

"Damn."

Nick didn't say anything else but then he was a man of

few words. He had a complicated situation with a father he'd never met and the inheritance that he'd left him after he'd died.

Nick clapped a hand on Gage's shoulder, sitting down next to him. "Your old man is tough. The toughest I ever met. He rode Marty hard and never showed any pride or offered any congratulations. Just always told him he could do better… Is he like that with you?"

What? He had no idea that his father didn't treat Marty like the golden child—the way he'd always talked about him to Gage.

"No. He tells me how good I am. That I was born to ride. Ah, fuck. He's making something up to Marty and sap that I am I'm trying to earn the praise he never gave me."

Nick didn't say anything for a long while. He shifted back to cross his arms over his chest. "I think about shit like this all the time when Reba brings up having another child. I mean I'm doing okay with Martina. A little girl who I can spoil, dote on, protect. But a son… Fathers and sons are always going at each other. Always trying to prove who's the better man and I'm not sure anyone can win at that."

"They can't. Or at least I can't. Sierra said I should only ride if I'm doing it for me. She said…well, just some stuff about not being able to fix the past and leaving it where it belongs."

"That's a good opinion. Only you can decide what to do," Nick said. "I'm going to tell you something and if you

185

repeat it I'll deny it and call you a liar."

Gage glanced over at the older man.

"I stand in front of Boots Kelly's portrait in the big mansion in Whiskey River and try to figure out why he would have waited until he was dead to acknowledge me and Xander. I try to get past the anger—which I still feel toward him—and see his reasoning. I can't. Reba said to let it go, but damn, I'd like to punch the bastard in the nose."

Gage laughed. He had felt the same way about his dad for a long time but seeing him sick and broken—a shadow of the man he'd been—had made his dad seem more human. Shown him he had feet of clay.

"I don't know shit about a lot of things," Gage said standing up as he heard his name called. "But I do know that fathers make mistakes just like sons do and maybe both of ours if they had it to do over again would make a different choice."

"Wise words," Nick said.

SHE'D PROMISED HERSELF she wasn't going to watch him ride. He was an ass and an idiot and he'd made it more than plain exactly how he felt about her, which of course did nothing to explain why she was standing in the Montez Denim VIP tent, eyes glued to the arena feed on the large screen. She wasn't the only one. All of the fans who'd purchased jeans and entered to win this VIP experience were doing the same thing.

The crowds were larger this week and everyone was in party mode. She wished she could be just the fan she'd always been but for her the stakes were higher.

The only difference between this moment and the first time she'd met Gage in person was that he wasn't just a hunky guy who turned her on. She saw past the tough guy bull rider to the real guy underneath. The one who was human and hurting and doing everything he could to get right with himself.

She understood that.

Really, she did.

But she also had come to understand that Gage had lost a part of himself when Marty had died and he'd become untethered. He no longer believed in himself and in Sierra's opinion that had led him down this destructive path.

She wasn't saying that he shouldn't be riding. Hell, he was very good at it. But she thought he should be riding for himself. And it had only been after their visit to his parents' ranch that she realized he was riding for Marty, trying to outshine him, and she started to suspect that his own welfare didn't matter to him.

And that had hurt more than she wanted to admit.

Falling in love with Gage and realizing that he didn't love himself was hard. She saw all the things that made him wonderful and a pain in the ass. No sense sugarcoating it. He liked to win. He was stubborn just like she was. But she loved him all the same.

And riding while he wasn't fully recovered just because his dad wanted to see 'Marty' ride in person again was foolhardy. It was beyond that. He wasn't going to get the satisfaction he wanted from his father. And by ignoring her, hurting her, he'd made her realize she wasn't going to get the satisfaction or the love she had wanted from Gage.

"I thought you weren't going to watch," Savanna said coming up beside her and draping her arm around Sierra's shoulders.

"I wasn't, but I can't help myself. That idiot. He'll probably be fine just to prove me wrong," she said and then laughed but felt it slipping toward that crazy laugh that happened when she was about to cry.

Savanna steered her away from the large screen and the fans. "Bruce, make sure everything goes smoothly."

Bruce nodded and Savanna took her hand and led her out back. The fresh breeze was warm compared to the air conditioning in the tent. It was a good day for bull riding and she'd been down this morning to look at the bulls, observing them the way that Gage had shown her.

Later there would be a big party that Montez Denim was partially sponsoring and all of their riders would be there. No matter how they placed. They had a special award made for Gage if he won. He was the closest of their riders to getting that top spot.

She tried to focus on the party. On what she needed to do tonight; but another part of her was just so consumed with Gage's ride, Gage's health, Gage's effect on her heart.

"I'm losing it."

"I can tell," Savanna said, handing her a bottle of water.

She took a swallow and closed her eyes.

"I thought when this thing with the two of you started that this was a good thing. You always have been wound way too tight and you needed to blow off steam. But this isn't what I had in mind."

"What wasn't?"

"You falling for him. Bull riders...they are tough and stubborn and sure, I'll grant that they are sexy as hell, but they live by their own code and most of them—especially Gage—have demons that they are riding to escape."

"I know that," she said. "But I thought...never mind. That's a lie. I know there wasn't much thinking going on. There was just a bunch of feelings. Lust, affection, laughter, frustration... He's doing this tour for his dad."

"That's pretty noble," Savanna said.

But Sierra shook her head. "No, you don't understand. His dad is battling Alzheimer's and when he looks at Gage he sees Marty sometimes. He's riding so his dad can see Marty and see Marty win."

"Well I can see why you fell for him. What is the problem?"

She shook her head, turning away. She didn't want to tell

her sister about Gage's battle with his dad. How this was the only way he could see pride in his father's eyes. That was too personal and she might be mad at him—oh, hell, but she still loved him.

She would probably love that big stubborn dumb-ass even if he never apologized for the mean things he'd said or even tried to win her back. Her heart and her soul had already committed to him and she was stuck.

She wrapped her arm around her waist and Savanna came over and hugged her tight. Her sister didn't say a word and Sierra appreciated that more than she expected. "Do you want to watch him ride?"

"Yes."

GAGE LEFT THE arena after his final ride. Holy fuck. He'd done it. No one had thought he could. But he'd had the ride of his life and he'd cut out his own tongue before admitting this but he was pretty damned sure he'd felt his brother's presence while he'd been on the back of the bull.

He'd had the best ride of his life. The bull was one of the tougher ones and when his points had been posted he'd known he'd beat Kane's score. Kane and he had been battling for number one all season. And the other rider had become more than a competitor; he'd become a friend.

He'd been stopped by fans who'd made it past security

and it felt surreal. Other riders congratulated him but it all felt like he was dreaming it—until he saw Kane at the end of the hall. The other rider gave him a bro hug and told him he'd get him next year.

He'd won.

Never had he expected it. Hell, he'd wanted it but he'd known how difficult it would be to get it.

Gage stepped out of the locker area and saw his parents waiting for him. He'd been surprised because his dad had been recovering from his fall off the Mule and Gage didn't think they'd come to Fort Worth.

"Congratulations, baby," his mom said, coming over to hug him, so close. Her arms started to shake and when he looked down into her face he saw the tears in her eyes.

"Ma?"

"Just me being silly. I'm so proud of you, Gage. And so happy you're safe," she said.

He kissed her forehead and turned to his father. Lawton stood off to the side looking at the floor rather than at Gage.

"I didn't know you'd be here," he said.

"We couldn't miss seeing our boy ride," his mom said. "Sierra arranged everything for us. Got us VIP passes."

Of course, she would. That's the kind of woman Sierra was. Even if he'd acted like an ass and hurt her feelings, she'd still take care of his folks.

He looked at his father and he saw that look of pride and love that he'd first glimpsed back in January when he'd come home. His dad saw Marty again and Gage realized that Sierra had been right.

Hell, she had been about a lot of things. There wasn't anything he could do to get what he needed from his father.

"That was some ride you had, boy," his dad said, coming over to clap him on the back and draw him into a bear hug. He held him tight. "I never thought I'd say this, Gage, but I'm proud of you, son."

Gage.

He knew that he'd ridden and won the tour. He knew that the he wasn't Marty.

Gage's throat closed and he tipped his head back to look at his father. "Sir?"

"You heard, boy. You did real good. I'm just glad I could see it," his father said.

"Me too," Gage said.

"Go get cleaned up so we can party!" his mom said.

Gage showered and changed. Making sure to wear the Montez Denim jeans that had been sent over.

He walked out of the hallway toward the fan area where he was scheduled for the last meet and greet of the season and he could hear the excited voices of the fans waiting for him. Hell, he was the winner. This was anything but routine and frankly he had no idea how to handle it.

Then suddenly that didn't matter. Sierra waited right outside the doorway for them.

"We will meet you at the Montez Denim tent," his mom

said, looping her arm through his dad's as they walked away.

He'd faced down 1,700 pounds of raging bull but that didn't intimate him the way that seeing Sierra right now did.

"I'm sorry," he said, making sure she heard it this time instead of mouthing it to her across the distance.

"Congratulations. Damn, that was some ride," she said. She stood there nervously and despite how shy she was at times nervous wasn't how he pictured his Sierra.

"It was, but it's nothing compared to the ride you've given me."

"I have? I thought I was a nuisance and should mind my own business," she said.

"I'm an ass. I told you that in the elevator in Dallas," he said, edging closer to her.

He might have won the gold buckle, the million dollars and the adoration of the fans but she was the only prize he wanted to claim.

"I love you and I hope you can forgive me for being mean."

She threw herself into his arms. "I love you, Gage. I can forgive you."

He hugged her close and knew he'd never let her go. "My dad knew it was me riding."

"He told me. Said he hadn't realized what a good man he had in his younger son until I pointed it out."

Gage had to laugh at that.

"Sierra, I know it's too soon, but I'm thinking about

marrying you."

"Good, I'm thinking about marrying you too," she said. "But first we let's celebrate this win at the party."

He agreed. This was the first time in his life that he felt something close to settled. He had his parents with him for part of the evening before Bruce from Montez Denim took them back to the hotel. He and Sierra danced and drank the night away and when he took her back to his room and made love to her, he held her close. Not afraid to let her know how much he wanted and needed her because he'd finally found something he hadn't known he'd been searching for. He'd finally found a woman to come home to.

The End

The American Extreme Bull Riders Tour

If you enjoyed *Gage*, you'll love the rest of the American Extreme Bull Riders Tour!

Book 1: *Tanner* by Sarah Mayberry

Book 2: *Chase* by Barbara Dunlop

Book 3: *Casey* by Kelly Hunter

Book 4: *Cody* by Megan Crane

Book 5: *Troy* by Amy Andrews

Book 6: *Kane* by Sinclair Jayne

Book 7: *Austin* by Jeannie Watt

Book 8: Gage by Katherine Garbera

Available now at your favorite online retailer!

About the Author

USA Today bestselling author **Katherine Garbera** is a two-time Maggie winner who has written more than 60 books. A Florida native who grew up to travel the globe, Katherine now makes her home in the Midlands of the UK with her husband, two children and a very spoiled miniature dachshund. Visit her on the web at www.katherinegarbera.com, connect with her on Facebook and follow her on Twitter @katheringarbera.

Thank you for reading

Gage

If you enjoyed this book, you can find more from all our great authors at TulePublishing.com, or from your favorite online retailer.

TULE
PUBLISHING

Made in the USA
San Bernardino, CA
06 May 2019